A LASS OF HIS OWN

A LASS OF HIS OWN

CECELIA MECCA

ALTIORA Press

To the greatest female warrior I know. Love you mom.

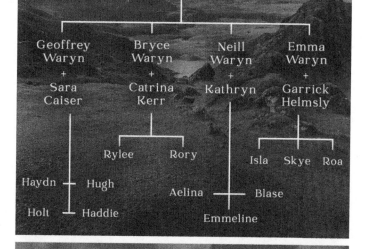

WARYN FAMILY

Geoffrey Waryn + Sara Caiser

Bryce Waryn + Catrina Kerr

Neill Waryn + Kathryn

Emma Waryn + Garrick Helmsly

Rylee   Rory

Isla   Skye   Roa

Haydn — Hugh

Holt — Haddie

Aelina — Blase

Emmeline

CLAN KERR

Catrina Kerr + Bryce Waryn

Toren Kerr + Juliette Hallington

Reid Kerr + Allie Bowman

Alex Kerr + Clara Wheaton

Rylee   Rory

Laire   Boyd

Orianna — Rodric

Galien

Ava   Breac   Conall

CHAPTER 1

GURSTELLE CASTLE, *Scotland, May 1301*

"Goddammit, Ranulf, you nearly got us killed."

Unrepentant, the man dragged the skiff ashore with Boyd and their other two companions. They'd been in this very spot months earlier, the stakes just as high then as they were now. All four men knew it, none more so than he.

It was Boyd's mission, and one he did not intend to fail.

"You wanted to avoid the English patrols," Ranulf said with a tug. "We take it in three, two, one . . ."

The men dragged the skiff ashore and into the same cave where they'd rendezvoused with the French that winter. Thankfully, Boyd knew Gurstelle Cove well. He'd come here as a boy—his father, Reid, had met once with the late earl.

Now, the earl of Gurstelle was dead. His wife and son, also dead. Only the countess remained, and without Boyd's assistance, she would meet her family's fate. But he wasn't here because his father willed it. Or even because the countess had asked for aid.

He was here because Wallace needed more men. Her men.

"I'm with Boyd," Robert, the youngest of them, said. "Those rocks were perilously close."

The skiff fully hidden, each of the men secured their bags and followed Boyd toward the path that would take them to a secret entranceway into the castle. Or to their deaths.

Gurstelle Castle was naturally fortified on three sides by massive cliffs that dropped into the North Sea. They would make their way to the headland under cover of darkness, to a single red rock wall accessible only by a secret entrance at its base at which none would expect four men to appear outside. To get there, they would navigate terrain that was treacherous at low tide. During the daylight hours. Now? It would be a miracle for all four of them to survive.

But Wallace needed more men. Freeing the countess from this siege would provide them.

"Since we speak of perilously close rocks destined to kill us," David, the other of the men, said over the sound of waves crashing against those very rocks, "you propose we climb . . . that?"

The moonlight clearly revealed their path to the headland, the small swath of land, their salvation.

"I do," Boyd said. Knowing a misstep could mean death, he stopped walking. Though he'd proposed it before, none of the men had taken his offer, which still stood.

"You've done your duty, gotten me here," he began. "Stay, wait for my return."

As always, the men scoffed at his proposal. "We go with you," Ranulf said without pause. He and Wallace had become close friends for a reason. Boyd had never met a man as loyal and fearless outside his own family before. Ranulf had been the first to volunteer for this mission.

"I alone am needed in there." Boyd gestured to the castle. "Why do you insist," he said to the men, "on risking yourselves unnecessarily?"

"I'd not face your father, or my chief, having abandoned you," David said. He was a Kerr clansman, one of a handful in Wallace's camp. And since no Kerr would leave another's side in battle, and David was the most loyal of men, Boyd should have expected his response.

"I go because they do." Robert smiled. Unbearded, like Boyd, his face was easy to see in the moonlight. Grinning, either unworried or uncaring about the danger they faced, Wallace's cousin was equally unmoved as the others.

"Besides," Ranulf added. "What if the Englishman accepts the terms and you lose? Who else'll look after your dead body?"

Now the men, having successfully navigated one dangerous passage to get to this spot and preparing for another, were having a bit of sport.

"Boyd Kerr?" Robert laughed. "Lose a swordfight. Are you mad?"

"I don't expect it," Ranulf said, "but if the Englishman is as skilled as they say . . ." He shrugged.

It had been Ranulf who first proposed the idea to Wallace.

To free Gurstelle's men to fight alongside them, what if they appealed to the baron's notorious skill as a swordsman? The siege of Gurstelle had lasted for more than three months. Rumors of desertion, English men at arms fleeing back across the border, had reached Wallace's camp.

"They say"—Richard took Ranulf's torch—"he was as skilled as Holt in the tourney, even as a young squire."

3

Boyd's cousin, Holt Waryn, was known throughout the isle, and beyond, for his prowess in the tourney.

"Was," Boyd said. "His time has come and gone. I've not heard of him entering one for some time." Though unusual to end a siege with a single duel, there was precedent. And if any circumstance was conducive for it, this was the one.

"If he takes up the sword against you, he will not win."

"And if he does not take up the sword," Boyd forged ahead once again, acknowledging his companions would not remain behind, though he'd been compelled to try one last time. "We can do little for the countess she's not already done for herself."

They'd discussed her situation at length, of course. Some were not convinced the stories they'd heard were true, that she held Gurstelle Castle alone. Most assumed that, with no husband or father to guide her, Lady Galia's marshal was truly in charge. Stories of her wiping the ramparts with her handkerchief after Lord Halton catapulted huge rocks against them were, undoubtedly, exaggerated.

And yet, Boyd had no doubt the woman herself led her castle's siege. He'd never met her. But when Wallace had realized he would be outmanned when Edward led this rumored attack against them, every one of his closest allies was tasked with one thing . . . securing more men. Unfortunately, Boyd's task was more difficult than most. The only approach to Castle Gurstelle was during a siege; one that risked their very lives.

Most assumed it had been because of their plan to challenge the baron to combat as a way to send the English bastards home, thus freeing Gurstelle's men for the coming battle, that Boyd had been chosen for the mission. But he knew it was not the only reason.

Boyd was not one of the men who questioned the countess's skill or reputation. How could he, with a sister who served as a spy for Scotland? Nay, he'd not question the capabilities of any woman, certainly not one who had staved off a man like Lord Halton, and Wallace knew Boyd was one of only a few men who could convince her to accept aid.

He would not fully trust her, nor any woman outside his own family.

But admire them? That he could, and would, do. Which was, aside from his skill with the sword, another reason Wallace chose him for this mission. Unlike Boyd, William had met the countess. And though he refused to offer much more than, "You shall see," when Boyd attempted to question William any further, he told him only to "come back with those men. Gurstelle is better positioned to aid this attack from Edward than any other, but they cannot do so held within their own castle's walls."

"If we do not survive this trek," David began. But Boyd stopped him.

"We will," he said as he looked out over the partially submerged rocks that lay ahead. He smiled at the men, daring the waves that crashed to shore to take them. "We must."

CHAPTER 2

"THAT ROTTING BASTARD." Galia paced in the hall's entranceway. She could see the servants watching her, listening closely, but did not care.

"What shall I do, my lady?"

Her marshal waited, patient as ever. If one of Halton's rocks landed at his feet, opening a crater that could see them peering down to the dungeons, would he react then? Though she appreciated his steady calm, there were times Galia would have loved for him to become as excitable as she did.

Which was perhaps the reason she wished for it. Simply because, no matter how hard she tried, Galia could not remain as calm as he.

"How could we crush it?"

Alan and his son, Lamond, Gal's sergeant at arms, exchanged a glance.

"Crush it, my lady?" Lamond asked.

She liked the marshal's son. Respected him. He'd even just married her lady's maid a mere sennight before the start of the siege. But there were times, like these, she wished for ingenuity from him.

His father, however, had been at this much longer. For many years, in fact, well before her mother, and even before her father, had died.

"'Tis currently in the moat," Alan said, "and unreachable by stone."

Though they'd known Halton was building a sow, having it positioned so close to the gatehouse was as disconcerting as she and the men had expected.

"We should find a private space to discuss this," Alan continued.

Galia met the eyes of one of the servants. If it was dangerous to say something aloud that was meant to be strategic, meant only for the ears of those who would carry out the counterattack, it was even more so to make her people feel as if they could not be trusted. To force them to wonder what would happen next.

They'd endured so much these past months.

"Nay, we can speak here," she said, deciding. "Tell me what you are thinking."

"I've not seen it done before, and am unsure if such a thing is possible . . ."

"If you consider it, then 'tis possible. Go on," she encouraged. "Explain."

Lamond seemed as curious as she was for his father's idea.

"We captured a catapult some time ago," he began.

She realized immediately what the marshal suggested. "Can you get it up there?" she asked, never having seen such a thing accomplished.

Alan looked at his son. "Aye, we can do it," he said.

"Will it reach their sow?" she asked.

"It will depend on the size of the rock." They now had an audience around them, the servants no longer feigning disinterest in their conversation.

"If you can launch one large enough to damage their sow in the right location, 'tis all that will be needed."

"Aye, my lady." Lamond immediately rushed off. What he lacked in intellect, he more than compensated for in ambition. Sometimes, the latter was more important than the former. Galia smiled, thinking how lucky she was to have both the father and son as a part of Gurstelle's staff. Nay, more than that.

Her family.

The only family she had, and one she cherished. Which was why the English bastards would not get through her gates. Gurstelle had not been under English control since her great-grandfather wrestled it from them, and it would not be under Galia's watch that it would change hands once again.

"Send a message to Lord Halton," she said.

He sighed heavily. Her propensity to taunt the man was Alan's least favorite of her tactics. "If you wish it, my lady."

She really should not smile on a day such as this one. But Galia could not resist. "I do. Will you tell him, please, to take care of his sow lest his men get injured in the care of it."

Galia expected the look he gave her.

But having forgotten their audience, she did not expect the round of applause her words wrought. She'd not said it for their benefit, but the servants needed the boost, as they all did, even if her confidence in their ability to eliminate this new threat was more than a bit exaggerated.

Part of winning was simply not giving up. If today proved a failure, so be it. All of Gurstelle would know, at least, she had no plans to capitulate to Lord Halton. Today, or any day.

"Very well, my lady."

That was Alan's way of saying, "I do not agree with you but will do it anyway."

With a slight bow, he walked away.

Galia adored the man, who was like a father to her.

She adored the servants who so faithfully carried out their duties despite no new supplies, despite the constant harassment at their gates.

One thing she did not adore?

Lord Halton and his men. Nor the English king under whose banner her attacker fought. She lifted her skirts, thinking of them both, and cursed the blasted men who puffed their chests and thought, simply because she was a woman, Gurstelle Castle would be the perfect fortification for their continued harassment of the Scottish borders.

Damn men and their self-importance. She'd had enough of it.

Enough of them.

CHAPTER 3

"Bollocks, Ranulf!"

Boyd had made it to safety, the sandy headlands beneath his feet more comforting than he'd expected. He'd slipped once and thought for certain he would fall into the dark waters below. Catching himself and seeing David and Robert safely ashore, he gladly sank his boots into the sand.

Until realizing Ranulf was in the water.

Thankfully, the moonlight aided his cause and Boyd jumped into the very waters he had tried to avoid. The men shouting both his name and Ranulf's was the last thing Boyd heard before submerging himself, swimming quickly to his clansman.

If the rocks didn't kill him, the cold of the water would. They needed to get out, now. Though Ranulf was swimming still, he struggled. Boyd grabbed him and pulled. They were not to safety yet. Keeping them both above water, the cold seeping into his very soul, Boyd stuck out his hand in time to prevent them from being carried too close to a rock. Pain shot up his arm, but he ignored it.

The sweet sounds of the other men and a sudden

tugging on his tunic told Boyd the shore had been as close as it seemed. They were upon it now, both he and Ranulf sputtering as they stumbled and were dragged ashore.

He stood, freezing cold with Ranulf, with David and Robert beside him.

"He's breathing," David said.

Ranulf was, indeed, breathing. Opening his eyes, he looked first at David, who held out his arm and hand for support, and then, after being helped to standing, he turned to Boyd.

When Ranulf opened his mouth, Boyd stopped him.

"Do not thank me for saving your arse."

Ranulf gave Boyd a quick nod instead.

But Robert apparently didn't understand. "Why should he not thank you?" he asked as the men began to walk, both Boyd and Ranulf wet and, if they did not dry soon, in danger still of having the cold take them.

"Because," David said. "It is expected. No man lets their clansman face mortal danger without aid, if it can be given."

"But he's not a Kerr," Robert said as they made their way to the castle. Though they expected no guards, Boyd watched the ramparts closely. As expected, none were on duty. At least not here, where only the maddest of men would attempt to make it ashore.

"We fight together for Wallace. 'Tis enough."

"I still do not understand." Robert stopped talking when Boyd held up a hand. He thought a shadow may have passed above them, the wall torches growing closer.

"We are friend, not foe," Ranulf said.

He'd apparently not listened closely as they rowed to Gurstelle Cove.

"Dead men cannot declare themselves," David reminded him.

If there had been the shadow of a guard, it had passed. Freezing and in need of a fire, Boyd was ready to go inside. As they'd learned, a door, well-hidden but blessedly, and recklessly, open, let the men directly into Gurstelle's dungeons.

He had never expected this part to go so easily.

Their original plan, if the door had been locked, as it should have been, was to wait until morn to be seen more clearly, to announce themselves as allies. But neither he nor Ranulf could afford to wait the night now, having been submerged in the sea. He was thankful for Wallace's memory of this passageway, but they were not safe yet.

Now to make their way abovestairs without being immediately run through.

"This way," Ranulf said, as if he knew the ground floor's layout. They had no light, and none was afforded to them by way of an arrow slit down here. Feeling their way through the musty, empty dungeons, their group managed to locate a set of stone stairs.

"Locked," Ranulf said, reaching the door first.

"I'm surprised these are unused with the enemy at their gates. Surely men from the siege have been captured?" David mused.

"Mayhap the Lady Galia is as bloodthirsty as she is cunning," Boyd said. "And they are all dead."

Though he meant it as a jest, Robert did not take it as one. "I'd not wish to tangle with her," he said. "From what Wallace has said of her."

"I would tangle with the devil himself for warmth," Ranulf said. Though Boyd couldn't see him, he could hear the man's teeth chatter.

There was no help for it. None knew what part of the castle the door they found themselves at led to. It could be night again, or days even, until they were discovered.

He pounded his fist on the door.

"Ahh, Christ," Robert muttered.

"Sheath your swords," Boyd said when he heard the telltale sound of steel. He continued to pound his fist on the wooden door, calling out now as well. With luck, it would not be long until he and the men were discovered.

Thankfully, they did not wait long.

When he heard the grinding of the lock on the other side, coupled with the sounds of men's voices shouting, he moved ahead of the others. If anyone were to take the brunt of Gurstelle's surprise at finding them here, it would be him.

As the door was whipped open, light blinded him momentarily. Even so, he held up his arms as if in surrender. "We mean you no harm."

He was pulled into the light. One by one, each of them were taken, their hands held behind their backs. Thus far, however, none of their throats had been slit. They were in a corridor, dimly lit by wall torches but light enough to see the faces of the men they now needed to convince they were not the enemy.

"There is a man in your service," he added quickly, "by the name of Alan MacCabe. Take us to him, and he will tell you we are friend and not foe."

"How did you come to be here?" the man holding Robert shouted.

"Who are you?" another asked. It seemed they all spoke at once.

"We come from Wallace's camp and wish to aid Gurstelle."

"They must be secured," one of the men said.

Boyd held back from answering, "'Tis a fine idea."

By the time they were finally escorted from the corridor, all four of them found themselves in iron shackles.

"Might we meet with MacCabe soon? My friends were nearly killed risking themselves to be here, and could use dry clothes and a fire," David said.

While Boyd appreciated the effort, he was fairly certain Gurstelle's men cared little if he and Ranulf met their deaths due to cold. Indeed, there was no urgency as they were led abovestairs to, presumably, Gurstelle's hall.

There were few moving about the castle. Most would have found their beds by now. But it was still well lit, and well appointed. As they emerged from yet another corridor, Gurstelle's hall before them, Boyd took in the bright tapestries. Overhead was a vaulted ceiling with wooden crossbeams, and swords of every shape and size hung all around them. He even spotted an axe similar in shape and size to his cousin's. Were they weapons of her forebearers?

"What in the name of all that's holy?"

Boyd didn't know the man that walked into the hall now. But his family did. He would be their saving grace.

"Alan MacCabe?" Boyd guessed as the man's eyes found his.

Angry and suspicious, his hand lying on the hilt of his sword, Gurstelle's marshal glared at him.

"Aye. Who are you? I'm told you came in through the dungeons. How is such a thing possible?"

Boyd had begun to shudder. Not from fear, but from cold.

"We came in with the tide and hid our skiff from Halton's patrols. I am Boyd Kerr, son of Reid Kerr and Lady Allie of Lyndwood. Though we are here to offer aid to

Gurstelle at William Wallace's command, I appeal to you as a member of the Brotherhood to hear our proposal. After," Boyd added, "we are unchained and provided warmth, lest my man and I catch our deaths."

As expected, his introduction caused a stir among the men. For his part, MacCabe already seemed less suspicious.

"Your uncle," he said. "The chief of Clan Kerr." As if Boyd were not aware of it. "What coat of arms does he wear?"

It was a trick question. "None. His own surcoat is emblazoned with nothing but plain black stitch."

"Why?"

"A practice he began as a boy when his father was identified and killed for it in battle."

MacCabe's suspicion seemed to diminish further. "A man your father adored as a young lad. What was the Frenchman's name?"

"Bernard."

"Your English family, as you say—the Brotherhood."

"What of them?"

The hall was silent except for Boyd and the marshal.

"Neill Waryn lost only once in all his years in the tourney. To what man?"

"His brother." Boyd smiled, despite the cold seeping into his bones. "It is a tale none will ever forget, as my Uncle Bryce ensures all know of his victory."

"Not all," MacCabe amended.

"Close friends and allies. You among them, apparently, as you asked the question."

Satisfied, MacCabe ordered, "Release them. Fetch a maid with dry clothing from my son's larder and take them to the Douglas Tower. Once dry and fed," he said to Boyd, "will you come back to the hall? The hour is late, but

Lady Galia will wish to learn of your presence. And purpose."

"Of course," Boyd said, grateful to have his wrists released. Then to his other men, "Find your beds. You've earned it."

None argued with him and all seemed grateful for the respite. For his part, Boyd wished only for warm clothes and an audience with Lady Galia.

With luck, by morn the duel would be set. The siege, over.

His stay here, brief and uneventful.

CHAPTER 4

"Shall I pin your hair, my lady?" Ada asked.

"When I am called from my bed"—Galia lifted her skirts—"at such an hour, the circumstances do not require it."

Ada gave her a look that said, *I agree.*

Galia's maid had been with her for more than five years, since she arrived at Gurstelle with her father, the new blacksmith. Similar in age, they had become more than mistress and maid. Ada was a friend, and as such, Galia had told her many times to use her given name when in her private chambers. But Ada's training prevented it.

"Do you think," Ada asked as she opened the door, "Lord Halton will be so discouraged after this night's defeat he will reconsider this siege?"

Galia smiled. Indeed, it had been a defeat for the ages. Never could they have imagined their plan would have worked so well as to bring Halton's sow to the ground. Or, more precisely, into the moat.

"We treat with him on the morrow and shall see," she said, not wanting to say more for fear the words may ruin what was Galia's most fervent hope. That the English baron would, indeed, admit defeat and leave their gates for good. If her mother were alive to witness this siege, she would be proud of Galia's efforts—of that she was certain—but also concerned. They were on the precipice of perhaps the closest Gurstelle Castle had come to falling into English hands in over a hundred and fifty years.

I will not be the one to lose it, and my head.

"Go back to bed, Ada," she said, leaving the chamber. "You should not have to remain awake for this."

Though admittedly, she did not yet know what "this" was, precisely. Only that Alan had sent for her, saying, "'Tis not the English, but your presence is required."

If their attackers were not advancing, Galia could not imagine why the marshal would need her at this hour. But she'd not hesitated. Ada had helped her dress quickly, but Galia was certain there was still a wild look about her, having been roused from bed.

No matter. Her marshal had witnessed Galia as a child with mud on her face after having eaten—yes, eaten—a worm. He'd been there when she cried for two days and nights while her mother, the countess, had died. Neither he, nor any of the men with him, cared if Galia's hair were pinned. Or her gown the height of fashion. All of the things other women her age coveted were insignificant to Galia. She cared only to continue her mother's legacy. Her grandfather's legacy.

"There is no need to follow me," she said to Ada, whose footsteps did not fall away behind her. The maid caught up to Galia just as she descended the staircase.

"I am as curious as you, my lady, and no longer tired."

"Lady Galia." A guard was positioned at the bottom of the stone stairwell.

Her chin raised, Galia straightened her back. "Something is amiss?" she said, ruing the casual pace at which she had come belowstairs. Now rushing forward, knowing there was more to this summoning than she first anticipated, Galia made her way quickly through the corridors of her castle to the great hall below.

Two more guards joined her at its entrance.

"They've moved to the solar chamber," one of the guards said.

"What is happening?" she asked. "I was told the English had not advanced this night."

"They've not," the guard said, gesturing to the back of the hall. Galia moved so quickly she left Ada and the others behind.

Alan sat inside, just to the left of the stone hearth, ale in hand, as if he were welcoming a guest. Indeed, she spied the top of a head in the chair whose back faced her.

"MacCabe?"

He bounded from his seat.

His companion did as well. When he turned to her, Galia felt as if all the air from the chamber had rushed into her chest.

She shivered.

Neither she nor the man spoke. It was as if he'd felt it too, the odd sensation, as if . . . as if she knew him. But if Galia had met a man such as he before, she'd have easily remembered. He must be nearly as tall as Longshanks himself. But unlike the English king, a man she'd met but once, the stranger was not lean. Nay, he was a warrior through and through. Even layers of clothing could not deter from the fact. Likely every inch of him was as hard as the stones of the hearth behind him.

But it was his eyes Galia could not look away from. They

bore into her, not seeming to blink. Alan cleared his throat, which was when Galia remembered there was a stranger in her solar chamber. One who'd not been here when she'd taken to her bed.

Her eyes flew to the marshal's then. He raised a goblet of wine to her, and Galia stepped forward to take it. "Who," she addressed the stranger directly, "are you?"

"Boyd Kerr of Clan Kerr," Alan said, by way of an introduction. "If you will sit, my lady," Alan said. Galia came around to an empty, velvet-cushioned chair. There were four in front of the fire. All winter this chamber had served as a war room where she, Alan, and their masters-in-arms met to discuss strategy and defense of their home. Once a place to conduct the most mundane of business, it had become so much more these past days.

As she sat, the stranger watched her. She'd often seen appreciation for her visage in men's eyes, but never once had she returned it. Galia would not marry. She'd not give control of Gurstelle to a stranger. Nor had she wished to relinquish her virginity yet, a fact that, if she were to remain a spinster, her maid oft said Galia should rectify.

There had been instances, brief interactions that had made her wonder . . .

But not like this. None like him.

"How do you come to be here?" she asked, the answer more important to her than his name. "None are to come in and out," she stated the obvious fact to Alan, "who are unknown to us."

His shirtsleeves rolled, this man was dressed simply. But as Galia looked more closely, she realized his hair was damp. Surely he did not . . . "Did you come from the sea?"

Before he could answer, Alan did it for him. "Lady Galia," he said to the newcomer, introducing the countess.

Then to her, "Indeed, he did my lady. With three other men, who now slumber abovestairs."

She leaned forward. "'Tis impossible. No ships have been able to get past the English blockade."

The man's smile was one of victory, but it lacked the kind of conceit she'd expected from one who, apparently, somehow, was able to avoid capture. As to why he was here, Galia was equally as curious.

"Not impossible, my lady." His voice, deep and thick with confidence of the like Galia had never heard. It was . . . inviting. Comforting in a way Galia wasn't certain she liked.

"How?" she asked. "Why?"

Ale in hand, Alan grinned in a way she'd never seen before, as if he were in the presence of royalty. Their guest leaned forward. Her gaze slipped to the open v of his linen shirt. Everything about him was hard, except his expression.

"We anchored in Gurstelle Cove, hid our skiff from Halton's men, and then climbed the rock coast to the headlands."

She stared, speechless.

"You . . ." Galia was uncertain she had heard him correctly. "Climbed the rocks? You could as easily have been killed as reached the shore."

He said nothing, for no words were necessary. It was a fact, and all three of them knew it well. "Why did you risk your life—lives—to come here?"

"We come from Wallace," he said. "We've knowledge of an impending attack from Edward. He plans an all-out assault on the last day of Hocktide that we mean to win. To do so, we need more men."

William Wallace. An impending attack. "My men?"

"Aye."

21

Galia glanced at Alan. Not surprised by the news, it seemed he knew of the tale already. "You may have noticed my men are currently indisposed," she said. Alan chuckled.

Their guest did not. Neither did he smile, exactly, but the corners of his lips did turn upward slightly. "We noticed, my lady," he said, his response as matter-of-fact as her own.

She was not one to fall prey to a man's visage, but Blessed Mary save her, Galia found herself staring at his lips.

"How then," she asked the obvious question, "do you propose I commit men to a battle when they fight their own? One I would gladly join," she added, "as any opportunity to thwart the English king is one I welcome."

Clearly pleased by her words, their guest took a sip of wine. Alan did the same, except of ale, his expression curious. He knew something she did not and seemed to be anticipating Galia's reaction. What did Boyd Kerr of Clan Kerr plan?

"My proposal is a simple one," he said. "Halton is known as an expert swordsman."

"He was well-known as a tourney knight, even here," Alan said, "in the borderlands."

"Aye," Kerr said, "and sits outside your gates himself."

"He does," Galia agreed.

"They say his supplies are low. His men grow weary of the siege and some have even deserted."

Galia looked to Alan. They'd heard rumors of the same, but those rumors hadn't been confirmed until now. It was nearly as good a bit of news as the knowledge that Halton's sow had been destroyed.

"We've heard the same," she admitted. "And I will admit to being glad to hear it."

Galia could not decipher his expression. Was it admiration? Something else? Either way, she refused to care on this stranger's opinion of her. And yet . . .

"I would appeal to Halton's hubris. Challenge him to a judicial duel as a means to end the siege."

Surely she'd heard him wrong. "You would . . . pardon me?"

"Wallace sent me to you knowing what I do, my lady. If he were to accept, I will win. The challenge would be getting Halton to agree. There is no risk to you or Gurstelle Castle. I can assure you."

So that was the reason Alan smiled then, and now, as if he were watching a musician play in the hall. But this was no entertainment. It was her home. Her people.

"Surely you do not believe I would risk Gurstelle falling into the hands of an English baron, risk losing my home, to the prowess of a stranger?" He could not be serious. "My family has held Gurstelle Castle for four generations. I would not see my people without a home, or worse, mistreated or killed, for such a foolish reason."

"Not foolish at all, my lady. Though the will of his men wanes, Halton's does not. 'Tis said he could be reinforced by Edward's men after the battle. Even if the English were to lose, they would bring enough men to find and close your remaining supply lines."

And they were down to one. Just a fortnight earlier the southern path had been discovered and blocked. Supplies now were slow and too meager for her liking. This news, if true, did not bode well for them.

"Even still, I must refuse your proposal. I'd not risk Gurstelle on the word of a stranger," she said bluntly.

"Then allow me to become a friend. We've little time to waste, my lady, if your men and I are to join the coming battle. But in that time, I will prove to you that a duel with Halton, if he were to accept, would risk nothing."

How was it possible for him to sound so certain of the outcome of such a duel? As if there were no question at all of whom its victor would be.

Unless he were truly that skilled.

"Why have I not heard of you before?" she asked. "If you are truly as skilled as you say? I've heard of your cousin, Sir Holt Waryn. And of Breac the Bold. But Boyd Kerr?" She was being blunter than she would normally, but the stakes were too high to be anything else.

Again, that half smile. Not quite a smirk. But something similar. "I've beaten both men of whom you speak, on more than one occasion. But unlike Holt, I do not seek glory in the tournament. And unlike Breac, I do not claim any title. He may be Lord Warden of the Eastern Marches, but to me, he is the son of my Uncle Alex. A cousin who I hold in high esteem. But also"—now he did smile—"one of the many men who've found themselves defeated by my sword. I'd not come here and propose such a means to end your siege otherwise."

How he could say such words without sounding as if he boasted, Galia was uncertain. He spoke as if his words were merely fact. So confidently that Galia almost believed him.

She had no intention, however, of agreeing to such an outlandish proposition. But instead of saying as much, knowing he would continue to belabor the point, she turned to Alan. "What say you?" she asked of her marshal.

"I say, tomorrow proves to be an interesting one in the training yard," he said.

An interesting one indeed.

CHAPTER 5

"SHE HAS no intention of accepting my proposal," Boyd said to David.

The sun had just risen, and thanks to MacCabe, he had his own clothes back, dried apparently by the kitchen's fire.

"You didn't expect her to so easily," David said. "With luck, she will not take long in convincing. What is she like?" his clansman asked.

Boyd was honest, as always. "Her reputation is warranted. Lady Galia is easily the most beautiful woman I've met. There is a strength to her that reminds me of . . ." He struggled to describe the countess's sharp gaze. Was it like his mother's, shrewd but kind? Or his sister, who was nearly always a step ahead of all those around her?

"She reminds me of my Aunt Sara," he said, decided.

"Because she holds Gurstelle as your aunt once did Kenshire?"

Aye, the women had that in common. Many years ago, his aunt through marriage had fended off her cousin, who attempted to claim Kenshire Castle, and its earldom, in the name of the king when Sara's father passed. She'd defended both, and all in Northumbria and farther south even, knew the tale.

"Aye, but there is something else about her." He thought of the way she listened to him. Looked at him. "The strength of her will," he said finally, "is much like Aunt Sara's. I understand easily now how she holds Gurstelle, and . . ." Boyd smiled. "I begin to believe some of the tales William relayed of her."

David made a sound that said he disagreed. "You truly believe she sent a freshly baked loaf of bread and French wine to greet Halton when he first arrived at her gates?"

Boyd thought of Lady Galia as she first entered the solar chamber. "I've no doubt the tale is true," he said. "Come. Let us break our fast."

With the aid of a different servant than before now standing outside their door, Boyd and David made their way through the maze of corridors belowstairs. Gurstelle, as its reputation indicated, was large for a border castle. Most here were built much smaller, to withstand such constant attacks and besiegement as Gurstelle endured even now.

Ranulf and Robert were seated already, but Boyd's gaze flew directly to the raised dais. She sat alone. Fitting, perhaps. Some might feel sorrow for her, a young woman with no parents or siblings by her side.

Boyd did not, however. It was pride, instead, that coursed through him. Pride for a stranger, but not for long. Instead of sitting with his companions, as he should have done, Boyd strode to the head table.

He bowed before her.

"Good morn, my lady."

Less disheveled, more polished than she'd been last eve,

Lady Galia was equally as beautiful this morn. And equally mistrustful of his intent.

"Good morn, sir," she said. "Apologies—I assume you hold the title?"

"I do, my lady. I was knighted by my uncle, the Earl of Kenshire."

Her chin raised. "An English earl."

"Indeed," he said, unapologetically. "Surely you've heard of the Brotherhood?"

"I have." She said nothing more about the alliance between Boyd's two families. More than simply intermarrying, Clan Kerr and the Waryn families formed a sort of protection at the border. A safe passageway for those traveling between two countries with friends and relatives on each side. An alliance that had, unfortunately, gained the attention of King Edward, who made no effort to hide his displeasure at the growing influence of the Brotherhood.

Boyd, knowing the question was bold, asked anyway. "Would my lady consider breaking her fast in private? I see you've not yet been served, and we've much to discuss."

As expected, she stared at his request. Even so, the countess considered it. He pressed.

"As you yourself observed, my men and I risked everything to be here. If you would but give us a sennight to prove ourselves. Then, if you wish it, we shall leave the way we came."

Boyd had no desire to do so. He'd prefer to leave Gurstelle out of the front gates, with Halton's men retreating south. But he would also do what was necessary to secure these men, win the battle against Edward, and continue to win the war he knew was coming.

She stood. Decisive, as he'd expected.

"Come," she said, taking her attendant unaware, lifting

her shifts to descend the stairs of the dais before they could reach her. "Follow me."

He could see his men's smirks from the corner of his eyes. Cheeky bastards. Having survived the rocks of Gurstelle Cove with them, Boyd felt an affinity toward them as he might his own cousins. Good men. With families who would never feel truly secure until the matter of a Scottish king, and Edward's increasingly harried role in the matter, were settled.

"Have food and drink sent to the solar," the countess said to a serving girl. Then, to another man at the hall's entrance, a steward perhaps, she said, "If there is any news from beyond the walls, bring it to me in the solar, if you please."

"Aye, my lady."

"For a castle under siege," Boyd said as they entered the same chamber where they had met the night before, "you seem little affected here."

She nodded to the guard, who closed the large wooden door behind them. As it creaked shut, he wondered at the wisdom of her finding herself alone with an armed man yet a stranger to her.

Today, they sat at a small table in the corner instead of by the fire. Since the fire raged, Boyd assumed this was where Lady Galia spent much of her time.

"We've provisions." She extended her arm, indicating Boyd could sit. His mother would take a leather strip to his backside if he attempted it. Instead, Boyd pulled out a chair for the countess. He wondered, for a brief moment, if he'd been too bold. She moved in front of him, her scent of a woman freshly bathed, and sat, offering her thanks.

Enthralled by her easy manner, it took Boyd a moment to remember to take his own seat.

"Though it's been many years since Gurstelle has seen a siege, the threat of it has been foremost in my mind. My mother's and grandfather's before me."

"I am sorry for your loss," Boyd said. "William told me of your parents."

"It's been many years since my father passed. My mother . . ." A shadow crossed her features. "More recently. She was a remarkable woman."

"As is her daughter."

Other women may have preened, or at least smiled at the compliment. Lady Galia did not. Which was just as well. Boyd hadn't said it to earn her praise but because it was true.

"Many thanks for your kind words," she said, not clarifying which of his words she referred to. Boyd assumed the first, and not the second.

The door opened.

A servant, the same one from the hall, put a wooden tray of bread and butter, along with a variety of fruit, before them. And ale, of course. She placed another plate before each of them and poured the ale. Bowing, she left as quickly as she came.

"Please," Lady Galia said, indicating he should eat.

Boyd did, but he hardly tasted the meal. He was too enthralled with the woman across from him. He wanted to know more. Which, thankfully, had been the purpose of asking her to dine with him.

"I offer only the truth," he said, matter-of-factly. "I was raised," he continued between bites, "hearing of my Aunt Sara's exploits. How she held Kenshire against her cousin and forced the king to allow her to break the betrothal that he'd arranged herself."

CECELIA MECCA

"I will admit," she said, "to having admired Lady Sara for many years."

That surprised him. "You seemed displeased when I mentioned my uncle earlier. I thought 'twas because he was English."

She seemed genuinely confused. "Nay. All know he fights for our cause. The Waryns are allies, and I know it well."

"Then why—"

"I apologize for displaying any displeasure. That I'm unable to hide my feelings is a constant source of irritation to those around me. I've just often wondered why women could not be afforded such a boon. To be knighted, as it were."

Boyd laughed, and then immediately realized she might mistake his reaction. "I laugh not because I think the idea absurd, but because it is so often a discussion in my family that it feels, in some ways, I sit with my sister now and not a stranger."

As soon as the words left his mouth, Boyd silently amended them. Nay, it did not feel like Lady Galia was a sister at all. The thoughts he'd had of her last eve while lying in his bed were anything but the brotherly type.

"Such a discussion is unusual," she ventured, taking a sip of ale. "Is it not?"

"Indeed. But my family is most unusual." He could not tell her, of course, that his sister even now was a spy for England. "My mother and her sister's upbringing made their courtships with my father and uncle more unconventional than most."

"They are also English, are they not?"

"You are well-informed, my lady."

"Galia," she said.

That she would offer use of her given name to him was a good sign. "Galia." He tested it on his tongue. "A most unusual name. For a most unusual woman."

Her laugh came so easily that Boyd wondered how it was the first he'd heard from her. "I will take your words as a compliment, sir."

"They were meant as one," he offered. "'Tis Boyd, my lady." He amended, "Galia."

"Boyd," she said, taking a bite of bread, her lips parting so delicately.

And yet . . . this was not a delicate woman. She was anything but, and Boyd could not help but admire her.

"All along the border know of your family, as I'm sure you are aware."

He did not deny it. "We've worked hard to eke out some safety where turbulence reigns."

There was a tension in the chamber that Boyd could only compare to that of the start of battle. Or the moment just before an opponent struck their first blow. A mix of emotions heightened by the very real threat of danger. Or, in this case, something worse.

For him, at least.

Unlike some of his cousins, Boyd had no intentions of taking a wife. He fought for Wallace knowing the path ahead of his fellow Scotsman was one filled with strife. Certainly not one to bring children into willingly.

"As I said, I know of Sir Holt Waryn, and of course Breac the Bold, but less of the others."

"Of me, you mean."

She smiled. "Aye. And yet you claim to have bested men whose reputations are unparalleled?"

"I've no desire to convince you with words," he said. "I

will gladly train with your men this day and prove to you they are more than empty boasts."

"You're not a man to boast, are you . . .Boyd?"

"Nay, I am not."

"'Tis the reason you sit here, with your sword still hanging by your side, alone with me."

The statement took him aback. "I had wondered at your reasoning for such a thing."

Galia took a deep breath, sat back, apparently finished with her meal, and grabbed her mug as a man might. "That my marshal trusts you, would allow you to lie in your chamber unguarded, says much. Even so, I've met few men I would care to dine with alone."

"I do not take you for a woman with a naturally trusting nature, Galia," he said honestly.

"I am not."

Their eyes met. She was saying she trusted him, of sorts, though why, precisely, he could not name. Perhaps the reason, and means, by which he came to be here?

"I will not misuse any of your earned trust," he said. "Indeed, I am here because I believe our causes to be intertwined."

"Though I'm not convinced of that," she admitted, "I do appreciate your efforts."

He smiled. "In nearly getting killed to be here?"

"Tell me," she said. "How did you and your friend find yourself in the water? Or, better, tell me how your other companions did not."

"We trained for it," Boyd said. "Spent a day in less, shall I say, adverse conditions. Keeping ourselves centered, treading carefully, each step slowly transferring weight from one foot to the other. 'Tis much like walking on ice."

"Your man fell, and you rescued him?"

Boyd startled. "Did Ranulf tell you as much?"

"He did not. But he seems like the sort to be more reckless, and you, the sort most likely to risk yourself to save another."

"Hmm." He was not convinced she had guessed that without being privy to more information than she admitted. "You ascertained that after such a short meeting?"

Lady Galia placed her mug back onto the table. "I have spent years fending off men, potential suitors and worse, surviving only by my mother's example. She rightly told me after my father died that our road would be a difficult one alone, but that we would survive only by listening more than talking. By observing more than acting. Her advice has served me well."

He'd met many, many strong-willed women. Often wondered if the lot of them had all found their way to his very family. Yet still, the countess managed to surprise him.

"I am not reckless," he finally admitted. "But will be so now, if you'll permit me."

Gal's eyebrows rose. "I am intrigued."

He would intrigue her in many ways if the woman would allow it. "There seems to be"—how could he describe it?—"an understanding between us. Despite that we are strangers."

She neither smiled nor frowned. "I will not deny it."

Boyd's heart hammered in his chest. This was no black ocean whose tide threatened to carry him away. Nor did he face a contingency of Edward's men prepared to slay him. And yet, Boyd's body was prepared for battle, nonetheless. Every muscle in his body, now tense.

"Watch me train, Galia. Know the truth of my words. And let me end this siege. If Halton will allow it, and I believe he just may, let me fight him and, once he is defeated, send men with me to defeat the bigger enemy. One that will continue to send more men like Lord Halton against you with no fear of repercussion until Scotland is free of his tyranny. Fight alongside me."

He appealed to her as she was, a warrior with a common enemy.

"I will watch you train," she said only.

It was less than he'd hoped for, but enough for the moment.

"If you'll lead the way, I am ready."

CHAPTER 6

SHE'D NOT SEEN anything like it before.

"How does he do it?" Galia asked. She stood with Alan on the ramparts, well above the training yard. From this vantage point, they could see the yard but also well beyond it. With the cool early-spring winds at her back, she wore a mantle, as did her marshal. Even so, after hours of standing in the same spot, the cold began to seep into her bones.

Yet she'd not move for anything.

From here, she was able to see Halton's men beyond the moat, camped out as they'd been even during the long nights of late winter, and this spot had become almost a solace for her. Though she knew they plotted, Halton switching from brute force to attempting to bribe or scare her guards to turn sides, it comforted her to see them mostly unmoving in their fields.

"It appears," she said of Boyd, "aside from being obviously well-trained, his lack of defensive moves makes such a thing possible."

One by one, Boyd defeated his opponents. The midday meal came, and went, and still he continued to fight all those who wished to challenge him. By now, with nearly every one of her men not on the wall in the yard, so many had lined up that he would fight into the night to meet them all.

"How does he not tire?" she asked Alan. Earlier in the day, the marshal had been as skeptical as she about Boyd's claims. Surely, he was a good swordsman to have been sent here by Wallace, chosen from all other men to challenge Halton. But this good? Neither of them had foreseen such a thing.

"Training, my lady. In truth, only by being accustomed to it could he last for so long."

"You and your men train when the sun rises, sometimes until it sets," she argued.

Alan shook his head in awe just as Boyd's sword ran parallel to his opponent's neck. If they'd been on the battlefield, her man's throat would be slit. His life, forfeit.

Now, it was not only Boyd's companions that cheered but her own men too.

"Perhaps he rises before the sun. Remains in the yard well past the time it sets. I know not, my lady, but can say one thing for certain. In my lifetime, I've not met a man more skilled with his sword than Boyd Kerr."

"Could he best you?"

Though it could be sometimes difficult to tell beneath his brown and white beard, her marshal's lips twitched. Could even be called a smile by those who knew him well.

"I will find out."

She'd known the marshal would eventually make his way to the field. All day he'd come back and forth, from this position, giving orders to the men both below and on watch, and she'd expected to see him at the point of Boyd's sword at some point.

"Today?"

"Nay, tomorrow. Or the day after, more like. When his sword arm is once again strong. I'd have no other reason for besting him than skill," he said.

Before coming to Gurstelle, Alan had been in the service of a clan chieftain so far north that he could see Torrisdale Bay in the distance. When the chieftain died, his son had relieved Alan of his duties, the man not half as honorable as the father and someone Alan did not wish to serve. Circumstances took him from the Highlands here, to the borders, where he met Gal's father. There was a wildness to his fighting style, even though he'd not been raised in the mountains, that could be attributed to his days up north.

Often he trained with the men, but she'd never seen a man best the marshal. It would be a disconcerting scene, one Gal might not care to witness, if Boyd managed it.

"If he bests you," she began, but then stopped. Surely such a thing were not possible.

"I would need the Virgin Mary herself guiding my arm for him not to do so," he said.

Gal looked up at Alan. "Surely not?"

He did not look away. "He would defeat Halton," he said with such surety Gal believed him.

"You've not seen the baron fight," she said. "His reputation—"

"Means little. Look." He gestured once again to the field. "He doesn't dance or parry. He doesn't hit out wildly or ever stand still. He interprets and stifles every attack and sets aside every blow with his flat rather than receive blows on the edge of his sword. I've seen none fight like him before, nor am I likely to do so again in my lifetime."

The compliment, from Alan, told her as much as her own eyes did of Boyd.

"To put Gurstelle's fate in the hands of a man we do not know . . ."

"We know his family. His cause. It is our own."

To put Gurstelle's fate in the hands of one man. I've spent my life proving I do not need one by my side to survive.

"I am unconvinced."

Thankfully, Alan did not spurn her words. If he felt strongly about accepting Boyd's proposal, he'd have said so.

Instead, the marshal was silent.

"None can best him," she mused, seeing one of her best swordsmen, who'd been on duty at the gatehouse for much of the day, overpowered by Boyd.

"Nay," Alan said. "They cannot. Ahh, or did I speak the words too soon?"

It was as close as Boyd had come all day to losing. Her man countered an attack meant to end the swordplay, but instead had twisted out of it and came at Boyd as the watching crowd gasped.

Even she leaned forward, Galia's hands covered her mouth. She'd become so accustomed to him easily winning that the sight of him faltering was made more of a surprise.

"He's tiring," Alan said. "No man can fight so many opponents forever."

She didn't want him to lose. Odd, as he fought one of Galia's best, and without highly trained men-at-arms, Gurstelle would fall into the hands of the English. If not now, another day when they were attacked. And that day would come. Gurstelle Castle's position so close to the border guaranteed it.

"Oh!" she cried as Boyd suddenly advanced. Indeed, as Alan mentioned, he never stopped. Never defended. Now, under his relentless attack, he claimed yet another victory.

She breathed a sigh of relief.

"Send word for them to end it," she said. "He's proven his mettle this day."

Alan actually chuckled then. Galia swore she'd never heard the sound before.

"I would say he did, my lady."

Bowing, he left her side. Another opponent stepped up, but this one was more easily handled. With a few flicks of his sword, both hands on his hilt, Boyd weaving back and forth as if it weighed nothing, the new opponent had been disarmed.

Her eyes rose about the field, above the courtyards and both its walls. Out into the fields where, from here, the white tents were no more than specks in the distance. Specks that were actually Englishmen looking to take her home from her. Specks that would kill her men. Kill her, if they had the chance.

Gal turned her back to them.

It was time, once again, to speak to Boyd Kerr.

CHAPTER 7

"My lady?"

Boyd pretended not to be surprised by Galia's presence in his chamber as he lay in the wooden tub. In truth, none of the women in his family cared much for the custom of administering to guests as they bathed, even those who were unmarried.

He knew of the custom, of course. Had his back washed by many a maid, and even more than one noblewoman. But Lady Galia of Gurstelle? The thought of it sent him deeper into the water lest she see the evidence of his desire for her.

"I told the maid I would be coming into your chamber. Did they not share that with you?"

She made her way toward him, grabbing a wooden stool as she did.

"Nay. But I'm afraid I made them uneasy. They left my chamber quickly," he admitted, trying to temper his reaction to her. In truth, if Galia thought to reach her hands into his tub, he was uncertain of his reaction. He was more in need of a woman than he'd been for some time, having

40

come straight from Wallace's camp, where he'd been training since December.

"Do you make a habit of it?" She indeed positioned the stool behind his back and took both the washing cloth and soap, as if she meant to . . .

Boyd stifled a groan.

She sat, her intentions clear.

"Scaring maids?" he clarified.

Galia did not reach into the tub. The scent of lavender, whether from the soap or the lady herself, taunted him.

"Aye. Shall I wash your back, then?"

Though his waist was covered under water, the rest of him was not. Twisting in the tub, he looked up at her. Cloth in one hand, soap in the other, she peered at him as any lady of the manor might. Not with the piqued interest of other women when they saw him in such a state, but as if he were her duty. Nothing more.

"Do you make a habit of it?" he asked her same question.

Her brows rose. "Attending to honored guests in this manner? Aye. Apologies if it is not a tradition to which you are accustomed."

She moved to stand.

"Nay," he said much, much too quickly. He tried again. "I would welcome . . ." *Your touch.* That he did not say. "Your attendance."

Their eyes met. Boyd willed more than she gave him, knowing 'twas a dangerous thing to do so. He was here for a very specific purpose, and wooing the countess was not it.

She returned to the stool.

"Do you attend to my companions as well?" he asked as her hand dipped into the water behind him. Boyd tried not to hiss out a breath. The thought of her fingers on him . . .

"I do not. As I said, you are now an honored guest. After your display today."

She left the rest unsaid. Not that Boyd would have been able to respond anyway. Her fingers now touched his back. Even through a cloth, they affected him as he might expect. Closing his eyes, he tried to decide whether it was best to enjoy the feather-light touch or think of something, anything, other than the fact that she was washing him.

"It is an honor," he managed finally as she moved from the middle of the back to his shoulders. "Though I am curious," he said, deciding on the former. Boyd lived with the very real threat of death on more days than he did not. If he were killed by Halton, or climbing back over those rocks, or en route to William's camp or in the upcoming battle, at least he'd have died a happy man. He decided to enjoy it.

Closing his eyes, he leaned back as Galia's cloth ran along the tops of his shoulders now. The lavender must have been her. This soap smelled of sage.

"Many women forgo this particular custom." He'd have said more, but Boyd found himself unusually lost. For words. For thoughts that were not scrambled in his mind.

"Because they do not wish to further subjugate themselves to a man."

As she washed, her finger slipped off the cloth and touched bare flesh. Galia may not have noticed, but he had. "Aye. My mother. My sister," he managed. "Most of the women in my family, in fact." He tried to remember if any had done it before.

"Many ladies of the manor are married," she said, continuing her ministrations. "And forgo it for that reason."

Boyd smiled, thinking of his father's reaction if his mother ever attempted such a thing. "Aye," he agreed.

She removed her hand from the water. At first he

thought she might be finished. But the fresh smell of sage told him otherwise.

"By my mother, it was done as an honor. She once washed the back of King Alexander, as a young girl."

"Did she?" he asked.

"Aye," Galia responded, her voice softer than usual. As if she was remembering. "In many ways, it did seem to me an odd custom. I rebelled against it until my mother explained once . . .when a woman rules in her own stead, she must use all means possible to gain an advantage."

Surely she had the advantage now, there was no doubt.

"Will you take the cloth?" she said, holding the washing cloth out to Boyd.

Once his back and shoulders were complete, it was presumed she was finished. But Boyd wished it were otherwise.

"Will you continue to my arms?" he asked. "It seems I can hardly lift them."

He didn't look back at her, but Galia did continue. Her cloth ran down his right arm. "'Tis difficult to believe such a thing after what I witnessed today. If Alan had not pulled you from the training yard, you'd likely still be lifting your sword arm to face another opponent."

"I would," he agreed. "As I told you and your marshal this morn, I would face as many of your men as you wished."

"And yet, you cannot lift your arms now?"

Boyd squeezed his eyes shut as her hand moved across his chest. He could sense her leaning farther over him. What he would not give to pull her into the tub with him . . .

"I cannot."

43

"Hmm." He could hear the smile in her tone. "How did you do it?"

She'd switched hands. The muscles in Boyd's left arm instinctively flexed as she passed the cloth over them.

"I was trained by my father as a young boy. Then later, my uncles. Each with a different style, but all with one thing in common."

She did stop then. Before Galia could move her hand from the tub, he grabbed her wrist. Twisted to look up at her.

Waiting for any indication she wanted to pull away, Boyd watched her features carefully.

"Ask me what that one thing is, Galia."

Her chest rose and fell. Her wrist was so small and delicate in his hand. "What did they have in common?"

"Respect." His jaw tightened, Boyd willing her to understand. "Respect for my opponent. For any who earned it, both in and out of the training yard."

She was anything but disinterested now. Her walls might have been higher than most women's, but Galia could not hide herself completely from him. When her gaze darted toward the tub, he resisted pulling her down to him.

Kissing the countess would not do.

"They taught you well."

His grip loosened. Boyd's thumb caressed her wrist for the briefest of moments before he let go.

"I need for you to understand that our desires are intertwined."

He'd meant to say goals, but Boyd's mind was as twisted as his words.

Her hand did not fly up from the tub when he released her wrist. Instead, it rose slowly. Reluctantly. As reluctantly as he was to see her leave.

"I will not mince words, Boyd." She could say his name a thousand times and he'd wish for her to say it again. "I've not seen anything like the skills you displayed today in my lifetime. But I've been sheltered here, my travels few."

Galia leaned down, grabbed the drying cloth, and dried her hands and arms. She laid the cloth on her lap.

"Alan has not my limited experience. He too was taken aback by your swordsmanship."

Boyd had been complimented as such so often, since he was a young boy, that it rarely affected him. He brushed it aside. Offered his thanks and moved on.

But from her . . .

"Let me fight for you." He had meant to say "for Gurstelle."

"I cannot."

Boyd was fairly certain he knew the reason. And it had naught to do with his skill or her fear that he might lose, both the duel and her home.

"Needing others does not make you weak."

He'd hit his mark. Another man might not have even known where to aim, but Boyd had been raised by Lady Allie of Lyndwood. One of his aunts had posed as a squire to force his uncle to bring her to safety across the border. Another endured a kidnapping after her home had been taken, and yet another, like Galia of Gurstelle, had stood her ground against foe after foe, facing down the king of England himself.

He could see her struggle clearly and would overcome Galia's hesitation. But not this very moment. He could also see she rejected his words.

"'Tis too much of a risk." She stood. "I leave you to your bath, sir."

As she walked beside the tub, her gaze once again

dipping to his chest, Boyd seized his opportunity. She would use any means necessary to gain an advantage? Then so would he.

Sitting up fully, he was exposed from the waist up. Galia did not even attempt to hide her appreciation.

"Many thanks for your assistance." He watched her carefully.

Galia's eyes met his. "'Tis my honor," she said. "I will send a maid inside to attend to you."

He pressed forward. "I've no need for assistance." Then he amended, "From anyone other than you, my lady."

Her countenance, so steady when she came into the chamber, was less so now.

"Sit with me," she said. "This eve, at the meal."

"Is that a command from the Countess of Gurstelle or a request from Lady Galia?"

She smiled. "'Tis both."

CHAPTER 8

"YOUR HANDS SHAKE, MY LADY."

Galia had left Boyd's chamber, received a report from Alan, and was now fully dressed for dinner. Her maid was correct. Her hands did tremble, ever so slightly, and it was for one reason alone.

"When I think of him," she admitted, speaking now to her friend and not her maid. "I've bathed guests before, many times."

"Never a man such as Boyd Kerr." Ada brushed her hair, preparing to plait it.

"Nay," she admitted, folding her hands together. "I stood on those ramparts and watched as Gurstelle's fate rested in a feat we'd never undertaken. Held my breath waiting to learn if that rock would stutter and fall into the moat or allow us to see another day, and yet, my hands did not shake."

"'Tis easier to find strength for others, less so for yourself."

Galia stretched her head around to peer into the clear blue eyes of a woman wiser than she remembered. "Ada,

47

'tis so very wise of you to say as much. I do believe your words to be true."

"Then 'tis you who are wise, my lady. I heard the words from you. Do you remember the day I confessed my love to Lamond? I'd told you of my intentions, wondering how, as all at Gurstelle know me to be a fine matchmaker, I was unable for so long to match myself."

"I do not remember them," Gal said. "Perhaps 'tis something my mother said." Before she spun back around, she glimpsed the maid's expression. "You do not believe so?"

"I do not believe every wise word you utter to have come directly from the late countess. There are times, my lady, where you must give yourself as much credit as all know you deserve."

Galia pushed her words aside. "What does a young woman such as I, who have been to fewer than five tourneys, only traveled twice into England and the same number of times north, know of being wise? I defend Gurstelle as my mother did before me. No more, and no less."

"Humph."

Ada surely did not agree. No matter. There was a more pressing issue at hand, and for once, 'twas not the siege. Since the sow had been destroyed, Halton's camp had been unusually quiet. The contingency Galia sent that day to speak of terms had been sent immediately away.

"He affects me like none before him," Gal admitted. "I should not have done it."

After his efforts that day, she'd thought to honor him as befitting his display in the training yard. Ada had agreed the idea was sound. But perhaps she'd been a bit too eager, too worried, too full of emotion to enter his chamber. In the past, she'd attended those who earned her respect without a thought. Always a guard remained at the door but never had she needed to call for one. Certainly there had been an instance or two that advances had been made, and she'd easily dismissed them.

But this eve?

"I wanted him to kiss me," Galia admitted.

Ada laughed. "Any woman who does not want that man to kiss her must either be married or blind, my lady."

But I am not most women.

She'd never said it aloud. But it was something her mother had instilled in her. These people were her responsibility. Her decisions should reflect their needs, and not her own. It would be a solitary life, as Galia's mother's had been after her husband died, but if she accepted any man as a husband, Galia could expect he would put his needs above her own. Above those of Gurstelle, which would be naught more than another property to him.

"We've hosted men before—" She stopped. Gal had been about to say they had hosted men whose visages were as fine, but that would not entirely be true. "Who proved themselves in the training yard."

Again Ada laughed. "In such a manner?"

Of course, it was absurd to suggest it to be so. Gal raised a hand as if asking Ada to stop.

"You may leave it down."

"As you wish." Ada came around Gal's stool. "Always you are Lady Galia, the countess of Gurstelle. If you wish to be simply Galia to him, you've earned the right."

Her heart sped up at the thought. "I've no wish for a babe," she said, already knowing what Ada would say. They'd had this discussion before.

"And there are ways to ensure you will not have one."

"Or for him to believe 'tis an indication of more. Most

especially with this particular man. I cannot leave our fate to him."

"Then tell him so. If he is the sort of man you believe him to be, his honor will prevent him from making anything more of your bond than you wish."

Could she do it?

Could Gal give her virginity to a man such as Boyd Kerr? She did not wish to marry, but neither did she wish to die a virgin.

"I will think on it."

"Do not think overly much. If you will not allow the duel, there is no need for him to remain. If there is a battle to come, he will leave soon to prepare for it."

Was she right? Would Edward's men battle Wallace, battle Boyd, and then reinforce Halton? If their remaining supply line were cut off, they'd not last into summer.

She thought then of Boyd in battle against the English. Clearly they needed her men or Boyd would not have risked himself, and the lives of his men, to be here. If they fought without Gurstelle's men, would Edward win? Boyd, be slain?

She shuddered.

"'Tis enjoyable, I can assure you. With a man such as he . . ."

"I think of Halton and not Kerr," she admitted.

Ada actually frowned. "Always you think of Halton. Of threats outside our walls. Of Gurstelle's crops. Of everything, and everyone, but yourself. I beg of you, just this once, can you not find your own pleasure?"

She blinked. "I am not certain," Galia admitted.

Again, Ada made a sound of frustration. "How can a woman as strong and brave as you find so little of that resolve for yourself? 'Tis maddening."

Gal could not resist a smile at Ada's impassioned speech on her behalf. She rose from the stool, took her friend's hands, and thanked her. "'Tis welcoming to know you care for me," she said. So few people did. Not for the woman, at least.

"Others would care for you too," Ada said softly, "if you let them."

Perhaps to some, the idea was a comforting one. But the thought of allowing anyone, most especially a man with such strength as Boyd Kerr, to care for her?

"I do not know if I'm able," she admitted, squeezing Ada's hands and then dropping them. "But perhaps 'tis time to find out."

CHAPTER 9

BOYD DISLIKED how easily he'd come to be at ease in her company. How quickly he'd shed the barrier of mistrust he'd built when the only woman he ever loved had been unfaithful to him.

Or, the woman he'd thought he loved, at the time.

Though it had been more than four summers since the day his sister came to him with the rumor, Boyd could feel the sting of Marian's confession even now.

"They will stand," Ranulf said to the others as they walked into the hall for the evening meal. "I'd wager an evening of ale at the Wild Boar on our return."

"Nay, they will clap but will not stand," David said.

"They're a reticent bunch. The siege has dampened their enthusiasm. I say they will do neither. He'll receive some stares is all." Robert slapped Boyd's back.

As the men wagered on the reception he'd receive after today's training, Boyd was distracted by thoughts of Marian. Of his bitterness afterward and his mother's despair over how it seemed to change him.

Shaking away the cobwebs of such an old wound, he

told the men what he thought of their game. "You are a pack of fools," he said. "I faced no true challengers today."

"There was one, near the end, who had some skill." David, who had called for the men to meet ahead of the meal knowing they might be deep in their cups after it, offered Boyd a crooked smile. Boyd found it difficult to know when the man was not jesting. Which was hardly ever.

"Not one of us could have done what you did." Robert winked at a pretty serving maid who walked past them.

"We're here for a purpose," Boyd reminded him.

Reminded himself.

"I'd not bed her, even if she willed it," Robert said. "I've a woman back home—"

He never got to finish. The others' laughter drowned out poor Robert's words. If he had a woman back home, he'd forgotten it last month when they traveled from Ettrick into England, stopping as they did at the Wild Boar. Robert had been the first to find company in his bed that night.

Boyd would have no opportunity to break a vow to any woman, as it seemed Robert had, though Robert was not betrothed, at least. He'd not put himself in such a position again. When he did marry—many, many years from now—it would be for advantage. An arrangement to bind his clan more tightly to another. He would care for his wife as he did the men beside him. Or Wallace.

No more. No less.

The claps began even before all four men entered the hall.

"Stand up," Ranulf whispered furiously to the gathered crowd.

Boyd shook his head. The men became so competitive with each other, even with something as trivial as this.

None stood, though Boyd would not have expected it. But they did applaud for him. Boyd cared little about that and more for the woman sitting alone on the dais. She appeared so small from here.

After the bath, one he refused to allow his mind to wander to again, he'd gone out to the ramparts. Watched with interest as Gurstelle's enemy moved among their tents. No doubt they attempted to bribe the guards, find her last remaining supply line, or maybe even worked to repair the sow that was ingeniously destroyed. The men trained, of course. And yet, from the ramparts, it seemed as if they did nothing but sit, and wait.

For Galia and her people to starve.

William had warned him, if the countess of Gurstelle refused his offer, or if Halton refused it when the time came, he could not linger. Boyd was needed for the battle that was to come. William knew Boyd's honor may prevent him from leaving Galia to face Halton alone once again if their efforts failed.

A warning, it seemed, that was necessary. Having met her, Boyd would no sooner leave her under siege than he would allow himself to act on the very instincts that had him reaching for her wrist in the tub. Until he regained his wits about him.

"She asked me to the dais," he said to the men. His gaze stayed firmly on the countess alone.

"Of course she did." David chuckled as Boyd wove through the trestle table. He acknowledged his reception with a few well-placed nods and even a smile for a young boy who sat beside, presumably, his father. A warrior whose weapon hung from his side as he and the boy sat side by side on the bench.

If Halton overtook Gurstelle, what would become of them?

At best, they would be forced to flee.

Galia's eyes were steady as always as she watched Boyd climb the stairs to sit beside her. She wore a gown of forest green velvet lined with gold thread. Her hair, unbound. "It seems I am not the only one here who thinks to honor you."

"Many thanks," he said to the servant who pulled the wooden chair out for him. Boyd sat, the applause dying only when he raised his hand in acknowledgment of it.

"Your people are kind," he said as the meal was served. Though not meager by any standards, it was one of a castle under siege. But Boyd did not need anything elaborate. He'd been camped in the wilds of Ettrick Forest in an abandoned stone keep with Wallace and the others for months.

"My mother treated them well. Many thanks," Galia said as her wine was poured.

"You speak often of her, but 'tis you who rule them now. Their devotion speaks to your treatment of them as much, or more, as the late countess's."

She was reluctant to offer herself the accolades she deserved. She was a natural leader.

"It was under her guidance that they flourished," she said. "I simply maintain what she has built." Galia took a bite of minced pie. They ate in silence for a time, both seeming content to do so. At least, Galia seemed content to do so. Every movement of her arm, to reach for a piece of bread or her goblet, Boyd noticed. Evaded. He was not certain how he had endured her touch as he lay naked in that tub.

His desire for her had been immediate and had only grown, alarmingly so.

"My marshal wishes to challenge you," she said.

He looked around the hall but did not see MacCabe. Likely he was patrolling.

Boyd's arm throbbed, but he would not admit it. "I accept his challenge gladly."

"He thought perhaps to give you a day to recover."

A younger Boyd would have spurned the offer. Told Galia he needed no recovery. But Boyd was less foolish than before. "I would welcome it," he admitted. "We expected to remain at Gurstelle a fortnight, but longer could put us in jeopardy of meeting Edward's men on the road."

"I understand," she said. "And still cannot guarantee the outcome will sway my thinking."

"Of course." She was not yet ready to concede she needed Boyd's assistance. He would understand the reasons. "You've held Gurstelle in your stead since your mother passed."

"Aye," she said, taking a sip. Though a hall of men, and some women, lay before them, it was as if he and Galia were alone. "And she for many years on her own," she said, seemingly knowing where Boyd was headed with his questions. "The thought of needing a man is not one I relish."

He hadn't expected her to admit the fact so readily. "Need is not the word I might use," he said, having already thought of his argument against her. "My Aunt Sara held Kenshire against her cousin's claim. When my Uncle Geoffrey arrived, she attempted to make him leave. From the tales they tell, she all but had him taken from her hall."

"Yet he remained?"

"Indeed. He'd made a vow to a dear old friend, the late earl and Sara's father, that he would protect her if Sara were not wed before he passed. Though she was betrothed, her suitor was in France fighting the king's crusade. You may have heard the tale . . . my uncle, having lost his home, had taken to reiving to survive. As you might imagine, the thought of a border reiver, and a stranger, arriving to 'rescue' my aunt displeased her greatly."

"Yet they married?"

"They did. My Uncle Geoffrey would say his wife was overcome by his charm."

When she smiled, Galia's features softened. As if she forgot, but for a moment, her many burdens.

"My aunt would say he seduced her."

Galia gasped. "Surely not?"

"Aye. If she were sitting here, she would say as much aloud."

"It seems they would recount the situation similarly?"

"Somewhat, but there are differences in the telling. Either way, the result was that he remained. Together they freed Kenshire from all claims and have ruled together since. In truth, my aunt is much like you. If she were here, she would compare my proposal to your relationship with MacCabe. Could you defend Gurstelle without him? Aye. Does it make that defense easier, to have a skilled man you trust by your side? Also, aye. The two are not exclusive of each other."

"Your aunt sounds as if she is a wise woman who furthered her cause by binding herself to a man worthy of such an honor."

Her words and tone were at odds. "You say that as if you are surprised."

"Mayhap because I am. Most men would not be content to rule alongside a woman who wishes to have as much control in that ruling as they do."

Boyd replaced his goblet, which was refilled immediately for him. "I agree," he admitted. "Most would not. But in doing so, my uncle began a precedent that is most unusual in our family."

"Unusual indeed."

If Boyd thought he was skeptical of the opposite sex, the countess was even more so.

"I ask only that you judge me not by the standards of most men."

Galia turned fully to look at him. Boyd met her gaze. "I could not do so if I tried. 'Tis clear you are not most men."

If his father had instilled one thing in him, it was that an abundance of pride could be deadly.

"I do not boast," he clarified. "Only to tell you of an unusual upbringing, one that may have prompted Wallace's decision to send me here."

The corners of her lips turned upward. "'Twas not your sword arm?"

"I am not the only man that could best Halton," he said.

"With so certain an outcome?"

He seized on her words. "So you are certain of the outcome then?"

"Ahh, sir. You've trapped me with my own words."

Boyd could not remember smiling so much with a woman before. "I did not intend to, but alas . . ."

She laughed. "I do not believe you."

"That I had no intention to trap you?"

"Aye."

"Or that I could best Halton?"

"I will not be entrapped again."

They were silent as the meal was removed. Boyd searched out his men in the hall. They paid him no mind, but there were others in the hall that looked up at him and the countess with interest.

"It seems to me," he said, more slowly, giving her attention once again, "you are not a woman easily trapped."

Galia prepared to answer him, but then seemed to reconsider. Her eyes narrowed, and now he wondered with great interest what she would say.

He leaned toward her as Galia did the same.

"I am not," she said, more quietly than she'd been speaking, "usually so."

Her eyes said more than her words ever could. The countess was as taken with him, it seemed, as he was with her.

The question now was, what to do about it?

CHAPTER 10

"Take that pot from the fire, you silly girl."

Galia pursed her lips, attempting not to laugh. The sun had not yet risen in the sky and the cook had likely already been lashing at the poor kitchen maids for some time.

"Margo." When she spoke, the girls suddenly realized Galia was at the door. They curtsied, Margo less so. "So kind of you to go easy on them at such an hour."

As she spoke, Galia attempted to break off a piece of bread. Her hand was slapped for the effort. The head groom's daughter, just old enough to be in the kitchens and new to such a duty, gasped.

Galia winked at her, letting the girl know it was quite alright. She might have been the countess, and Margo the cook, but the fact hardly mattered. Margo had served her mother and father before that. She'd even served her grandfather as a young girl.

Margo was Gurstelle, as much or more than Galia herself.

"I'll go more kindly when they listen. She's bound to get herself maimed before long."

Though Margo glared at the serving maid in question, she turned and gave Galia a very different look. One more kindly than the cook would let on. She liked to be seen as stern; her kitchen ran smoothly because of it.

But Galia knew the truth.

Her cook was as soft as the puppy she'd once had. When he'd become sick, it was Margo who stood beside Galia at his grave. That was just a sennight after her mother had passed, and the grief of it was too much to bear. That day Margo had taken Galia into her embrace for what seemed like half the day. She spoke of something she never, ever, had before.

The loss of her infant daughter.

It was through their shared grief that Galia and Margo had grown even closer than before. If a day passed that she did not visit the kitchens, as had been the case these last few, Galia felt as unsettled as she did staring at those blasted white tents.

"If you're wanting freshly baked bread, my lady, you best hie yourself up to the hall. Trays of it are on their way there already."

"Is not that a loaf of bread?" Galia indicated the loaf she'd attempted to break a piece from.

In response, Margo glared at another of her maids. "Aye, from a batch without salt. It'll curl your toes to taste." She turned back to Galia.

"Go easy on her," she whispered, the groom's daughter too far away to hear. "She's young yet and does not know her way."

"Go easy on her." Margo repeated the words as if they were blasphemy. Galia nodded to the kitchen's entrance.

Understanding, Margo followed, wiping her hands on her apron.

"Are you here to tell me of the swordsman?"

Galia's eyes widened. "How could you know such a thing?"

Margo made a face. "I know all there is to know at Gurstelle. And even if it weren't so, 'twould be difficult to ignore their chatter"—she waved her hand into the kitchen —"about him. Is he as handsome as they gossip about?"

That was the reason she was here. After supper last eve, after Boyd had retired, she could not sleep. For the first night in many days, she stared at the canopy above her bed, thinking not of Halton's men but of their conversation at supper. Of that bath, which, she realized, had been a folly to undertake. She thought of him in the training yard, relentlessly slashing away at opponent after opponent.

Sleep eluded her. Finally, after a brief and fretful rest, she arose and came below to speak to Margo.

Galia nodded.

Margo, who knew her well, seemed to immediately understand. "And as skilled with the sword?"

She nodded again.

"They say he came through the rocks at Gurstelle Cove and wishes to challenge Halton in a duel."

"As always, the gossip that has reached your ears rings true. He is a Kerr, come from Wallace's camp to ask for me for an upcoming battle."

That news surprised her. "Battle?"

"With Edward's men. But that, if it pleases you, stays between us."

"It pleases me to learn that bastard of a king will see another defeat."

"A scenario that is more likely if we are able to send men."

Margo made a most unladylike sound. "I've seen Kerr fight. Edward will be defeated."

That surprised her. "You've seen him? But you asked—"

"If he's as handsome and as skilled as they say, aye. I wished for your answer, my lady." Margo smiled, the many wrinkles on her face multiplying as she did. "I've my own opinion already."

Galia's hand flew to her hips. "You were in the training yard," she accused.

Margo shrugged. "For a wee bit, aye. Word of his exploits reached the kitchens. I'm an old woman, but widowed, and have still plenty of eyesight to appreciate a man such as he."

"Margo!"

"Ahh, that girl is lucky I like her father," she said as an iron pot clanged to the floor inside the kitchens. "Your bread is gett'n cold abovestairs, my lady." Margo's eyes narrowed. "Or did you come down here for another reason than to snatch it warm from me?"

Margo knew her as well as anyone at Gurstelle.

"I did," she admitted.

Margo waited. Galia said nothing. She was accustomed to knowing her mind. Even in matters that others might consider a man's realm. Her mother had ensured there was naught—not the castle's accounting or defense—she did not learn.

Except this one thing.

"You know my mind on this."

Margo, thankfully, guessed the direction of her thoughts. "To claim you want no husband at such an age . . ." Margo shook her head. "'Tis folly, if yer asking."

"I do not wish to marry him," she said, knowing Margo's mind well, for she'd said it many times. Even when

Galia's mother was alive, the two women discussed the matter for Galia to listen. Margo had told the countess, woman to woman, that she'd been wrong to counsel Galia so. That because her husband had been weak, the match not for love but for land, did not mean Galia should go unwed.

But in the end, the countess was her mother. Margo, her cherished cook and friend, was a woman who had not the burden of an estate such as Gurstelle to keep safe.

"You wish to bed him?"

"Margo," she whispered furiously. Though they could not be overheard, to hear it said so . . .

"'Tis not so?" Margo stepped once again to the side to yell into the kitchens. "Enough whispering, get you to working!" She frowned.

"Go easy on them," Galia said, knowing her words would not be heeded. Margo was not a cruel woman. In fact, she loved those girls as if they were her own.

"Well?" Margo asked. "Are my words false?"

Galia swallowed, unwilling to say it aloud. "I've not met a man like him before. When he is near . . ." She trailed off.

"Desire, 'tis all. And understandable too. I've seen more than seventy summers and haven't met a man like him before either."

"Your husband—"

Her laugh was closer to a cackle, but it soothed Galia's soul nonetheless. "Was a dear old man when he left me, an untried boy when we met. But he was no Boyd Kerr, my lady, and anyone with eyes will say 'tis so."

Galia made a face that Margo dismissed.

"I told you once before," she continued. "To prevent a babe—"

"I didn't come to ask for that," she cut in. "You've advised me well on the matter."

Margo's arms folded in front of her. "Then why are ye here? Say it plainly, Galia."

The use of her name meant Margo was losing patience with her. Understandable, since Galia was having difficulty forming an actual question.

"I'm here to know . . ." She swallowed. "Ada does not think I will go to hell since I don't intend to marry, but I do not wish for it."

Margo all but rolled her eyes. "You are a young maid who has not been kissed even once. Whose mother"—she crossed herself—"God rest her soul, was so worried for you to be free from the constraints of domination that she considered not the woman, only the future countess. You are in hell already, my lady, and do not know it."

Before Galia could think fully on the cook's words, Margo added, "Have I not told you of the pleasure that awaits you in the marriage bed?"

Margo was as free with her talk of pleasures as she was orders for the kitchen maids.

"The marriage bed, aye. But 'tis no marriage bed I speak of."

"If you truly do not wish to marry—"

"I do not."

Margo surprisingly had no quick comeback for her. Instead, the cook seemed . . . sad. As if she mourned for a marriage Galia would never have. Yet she did not mourn for it herself. She would wish for children, aye. And someday might rue the fact that she had no heir to pass Gurstelle to. Or babe to swaddle. Or young face to kiss.

But she'd thought of a solution already. Galia would pass Gurstelle to one worthy of it. What did she care if they were of her blood? Men cared more for such things, but Galia desired most to ensure those alive now were well taken care of. The future would dictate itself.

"If you are sent to hell for finding pleasure with a man who is not your husband, then your company will be great. You hurt none, my lady, if he agrees to such a thing. But to think of Gurstelle not knowing the pattering of children's feet..."

They'd had this discussion many times. Galia knew well Margo's position on the matter. "If that is the price Gurstelle must pay for seeing 'tis well taken care of while I live, then so be it. If we can withstand this siege, then surely we can hold off any other threats."

"It seems to be you've the means to end it if Halston will agree."

Galia would not discuss it. She did not need Boyd to save her.

Boyd. He would be in the hall even now. At her marshal's request, Boyd would rest his sword arm this day and challenge him on the morrow. She'd offered to show him Gurstelle in truth, and their tour would begin soon.

"By the flush on your cheeks, it seems you have your answer and path forward. And I've maids to tend to," Margo said as Galia attempted to recompose herself. 'Twas difficult now that she had made a decision, as Margo currently guessed.

She would not pursue him, but if Boyd pressed his suit...

"Thank you for your counsel," she said. Margo curtsied so hurriedly most would have missed the motion. But Galia did not. Though the lines of servitude and friendship were blurred, some of the servants counting as Galia's most trusted, they continued to treat her very much as the countess here. A fact that she could never forget. Galia was responsible for the people of Gurstelle, and nothing else, including her own desires, mattered to her more.

Despite the reminder, she found her feet moving up the stairs to the hall more quickly than usual.

CHAPTER II

"This way," Galia said, and Boyd followed her into the courtyard.

After breaking their fast, Galia met with the marshal briefly as Boyd watched his men train. Resting his arm at her man's request, one he readily accepted when he could barely raise it this morn, he walked about the men asking questions, which were answered freely.

His family's reputation had some benefits, including that of being more readily trusted than he would have otherwise been. Boyd learned one thing above all others that morn.

His admiration of Lady Galia was not misplaced.

Apparently, like her mother before her, the lady of Gurstelle was as vigilant in matters of defense as of food stores and accountings, making this castle formidable enough to hold out during a siege that may have broken weaker men.

Or women.

They cared for her, as they had her mother, and spoke little of the late earl. Boyd learned also that none seemed overly worried they would not prevail. The confidence in their countess to send Halston packing was admirable, if a touch misguided. With just one supply route undetected, her hold was likely as tenuous as any ruler Gurstelle had seen since its building.

Boyd also learned that, if he were to duel with the Englishman and prevail, the men of Gurstelle would readily fight for Wallace. They were as eager as him to defend against any attack King Edward could send against them. While supporters of Balliol and Comyn were as plentiful as those of Robert the Bruce, none agreeing on who should rule Scotland once freed from English oppression, all seemed willing to support Wallace.

Like him, they knew William Wallace's heart to be true, his desire not for power but to be free from Edward's grasp around each of their collective throats.

"Those buildings are new," Galia said, continuing a tour that should have been as innocuous as any he'd received from hosts in the past. But it was not. Boyd had not dreamt of other hosts. Had not groaned aloud upon waking, realizing his dream was nothing but that. He'd never entered a hall before with as much anticipation as he would have for delivering the English king's men to hell.

"When was the original keep constructed?"

She turned to look at the building they'd just left. "More than four hundred years ago by Myrddin Wyllt, a bard who was later knighted, as a stronghold for his family. As you can imagine, it has changed hands many times since coming into my family with my great grandfather, who was given the abandoned keep, by then a castle, as a reward for his service to the Scottish king."

They walked through the courtyard, the day as mild as any in recent memory, toward the east steps and away from the mid tower. The barbican was more fortified than any other location around the wall, a reminder that Gurstelle was a castle under siege. But they walked in the opposite direction.

"How did your mother come to rule?" he asked, knowing only some of the late countess's story. "She was not pressured to marry by the crown?"

She gave him such a look that Boyd could not help but laugh.

"Of course she was. As I am. But neither she, nor I, have the desire to give control of our people's fate to a man."

"The law favors you little. But you do not intend to marry?"

He could not remember meeting a woman before who'd said as much. Even his sister, who heartily resisted his parent's matchmaking attempts, was resigned to such a fate eventually.

"Do you intend to marry?" she asked as they climbed the exposed stone stairs in front of them.

"Perhaps. My place is at Wallace's side now, however."

"Yet none would question you if you said nay."

"My parents would, for certain."

"Your cousins? Your companions? They would not."

"I disagree," he said. "Even now, as one by one my cousins wed, they taunt me and those not yet having entered into such a state."

"Hmm." She clearly did not agree with him.

They stepped onto the ramparts, the North Sea in front of them, no guard to be found. Though it was to their advantage, he wondered at the fact.

"There are no guards here?" he asked, the wind whipping now at them. Though Boyd did not mind. The air, the sound of waves crashing upon the rocks . . . one could almost forget the threat at Gurstelle's back.

"None have come ashore this way." She peered at him. "Until you and your men."

Boyd took off his mantle. Though it was not as thick as some—their route here necessitated carrying few belongings—his companion wore none. Her velvet gown could not possibly stave off a chill that only the ocean's breeze could bring.

When he took a step toward her, his intention obvious, she did not move. Boyd reached behind her, and covered Galia with not a word between them. As he closed the clasp at her neck, Boyd resisted the urge to allow his fingers to linger. To splay his hand along the curves of her neck, pulling her toward him.

She watched him, still saying nothing.

"You wear no jewels," he noticed, his hands dropping to his side. Even still, he did not move away from her.

"I've little need for them," she said.

"A countess who wears no jewels and will not marry. I cannot say I've met anyone like you before, Galia."

"Nor I you."

He could kiss her. Wanted to kiss her. Boyd wanted to do more than that, but he was not at Gurstelle to woo the woman before him.

Though he'd not kiss her, Boyd could not resist making some sort of contact. Her touch in the bath was seared now in his mind, and he wished for that again.

His hand raised, as if on its own accord. When it reached her cheek, he nearly closed his eyes at the softness of her. So smooth and delicate, at odds with her countenance. Even now Galia's eyes blazed. But she did not pull away.

He allowed his thumb to run softly toward the edge of her mouth, where it paused.

"You are as strong as any woman I've known," he said. "And in my family, there are many."

Her hand rose and covered his own. Boyd groaned softly then. He could feel his body leaning in toward her.

"And you, as any other man."

"Why do you allow this of me?"

"I allow it because . . ." She stopped. Her fingertips moved delicately along his hand. "Because of the way you look at me now. Because you came upon our shore on those rocks below. Because you bested all of Gurstelle's most worthy competitors. And because you are not afraid of a woman wielding the power that I do here."

He'd not deny it. "Afraid," he repeated, his thumb inching toward the corner of her lips once again. This time, it moved even farther, to touch her bottom lip. "'Tis the quality in you that most intrigues me."

Her eyes dipped to his lips.

Galia wanted him to kiss her. There was no reason to resist.

The bang coming from behind them was so loud, so sudden, that when their hands flew apart, Boyd did not hesitate. The last thing he saw before he scooped Galia into his arms was the look of fear in her eyes.

CHAPTER 12

WHEN SHE REALIZED she was still wrapped in Boyd's arms, Galia pushed gently on his chest. His look of apology was unnecessary. But she had no time to discuss it as they both ran from the ramparts down a flight of stairs and then back up to where they could walk to the gatehouse.

A cloud of smoke blanketed an area to the east of the gatehouse near the outer curtain wall. Men scrambled toward that area as she approached.

"MacCabe?" she shouted, as men in arms pointed him out. With Boyd behind her, she found him directing some toward the smoke and others into the gatehouse.

"My lady?" He was surprised to see her and not at all pleased. "Get her inside," he shouted to Boyd, who looked all too happy to fulfill the request.

"What is happening?" she demanded, not leaving her spot until she had the answer.

"Naught more than a small pebble that managed to reach the outer wall. We will assess it and report to you immediately. Now," he repeated. "Go."

Another loud bang, though not as startling as the

first, underscored his request. Reluctantly she left the wall and made her way back to the courtyard with Boyd. "Go inside," he said, "I will learn what I can and find you."

Though her anger was not at him, Boyd seemed to take it so as they locked gazes. She reached for his arm before he turned to leave. "I rue only that I cannot aid as well. The baron is outside these walls, commanding his men, and I cower inside my hall."

Boyd looked from her back toward the gatehouse. "I will put a sword in your hand and teach you to use it, if you desire. But this day, I implore you, get inside now."

He did not wait for a response but instead turned and ran. Galia had no choice but to obey. Few remained inside the courtyard now. Most had found cover, and indeed, as she entered the keep, it was full of those who had left to come inside. Servants, women, children.

"'Tis well enough," she called to them. "Come, we will begin the midday meal early." She directed servants to reposition the trestle tables that had been moved to the sides of the hall. Touching nearly everyone she passed on the arm or shoulder, soothing as many as she could, Galia made her way through the back entrance of the hall down to the kitchens.

Very different from the lively atmosphere of before, the girls now appeared scared. She quickly reassured them. "All will be well," she said, catching Margo's eyes. "If we can send above all that is ready for the midday meal, many would be appreciative of the distraction."

"As you bid, my lady," Margo said, attempting to send Galia away, but she ignored the cook. Their food would soothe those in the hall, and Galia would offer aid where she could. She began to work, mindful of the gaping stare of the new kitchen maid. Others had seen her assist Margo before and seemed unbothered but also grateful.

Another lesson from her mother.

She may be the countess, but if she did no other job than order others about, Galia would never truly understand their work. Following her mother as a child from the kitchens to the blacksmith's shop, back into the keep to look at ledgers in her solar, neither remained in one place for very long. To this day, Galia had difficulty doing so.

"Have you a report yet, my lady?"

Margo's way of asking what had happened.

"Nay," she said. "But it appears to be a gift from their trebuchet to our outer wall near the east corner."

The cook nodded and continued to work beside her. Keeping her hands moving took Galia's mind from the very real threat that sat outside their walls and had now for far too long.

Perhaps you should allow it.

"Lady Galia."

The deep voice near the kitchen's entrance sometime later so startled her, and the others, that her fingers faltered.

"You'll cut yourself for certain," Margo said, glaring at Boyd, who filled the entranceway with his frame. "Here." She took the knife from her. "See to him."

Galia wiped flour dust from her hands on a cloth and would have smiled at the girls' expressions if the situation were not so dire. Each and every one of them, Margo included, looked at Boyd as if they'd never seen a man before.

For certain, they likely had not seen one such as him.

"If I might speak with you," he said as she approached.

Galia disliked the feeling of wanting to be wrapped up

in his arms once again. He'd done it so quickly, without thought. Protected her, though Galia did not need protection.

They moved to the same spot where she and Margo had spoken earlier. Galia, remembering the topic of that conversation, glanced back at Margo just before she and Boyd turned the corner. Unsurprisingly, the cook winked at her.

"It is as MacCabe said. A larger rock than usual reached the wall and found its mark. The second, much smaller."

"And the damage?"

He smiled. "More bluster than effect," he said. "Though it will take time to repair, and another of that size could be problematic, even now MacCabe is ordering a counterattack. If that trebuchet still stands by nightfall, I will be surprised."

She let out a breath. "So we've escaped the worst of it?"

"For now."

Their eyes met. Galia knew what he was asking, but she could not give it. "If you were to lose—"

"I will not."

She agreed. But even still. "'Tis my duty to protect these people."

"Which you will do by sending Halton's men from your walls."

"And if he accepts but still does not leave?"

"Then you will slice the throats of those he sends as assurance."

"Will we not need to send the same? Someone, or more than one someone, will risk themselves as assurance if we were to lose the duel. Could he not simply kill them if he indeed fails?"

"He could not," Boyd said. "For the baron would be dead."

A fluttering in her stomach that had begun when she first heard his voice persisted. But it was not anticipation, but dread now that Galia battled. "The duel is to the death?"

"Of course," he said as if they spoke of his possible demise as well.

"Nay." She shook her head. "Nay," she repeated. "I will not have it. Nay."

"You would grieve for the man who attempts to take Gurstelle from you?"

"Nay," she said again. "I would mourn for you."

For a moment, she thought he would reach for her. Mayhap kiss her. Instead, Boyd smiled so slowly and secretly that his eyes actually twinkled with merriment. "You'd not," he said, "because I would be victorious."

"You are so certain that you would risk your life to prove it?"

"I'd not be here otherwise," he said, matter-of-factly, as if stating that Gurstelle's wall had been attacked that day or that the sun had risen. "I did not mean to take you from your duties."

When his hand reached out, Galia's breath caught. Wiping flour from her sleeve, he pulled it back again.

Unfortunately.

"Did Alan say aught else?" she asked to cover the silence. Or more accurately, her warring emotions whenever Boyd stood so close to her.

"That he will offer a full report later. You've a meeting with him each day, it seems?"

"I do."

"I'd not take you from your duties," he said. "Please." Boyd's hand extended toward the kitchens.

"I would assure them that all is well and"—she had a

thought—"continue our tour? It would bode well for me to be seen, to reassure all those who may be scared."

Boyd inclined his head in acquiescence with her plan.

She was quick about the telling in the kitchens, not wanting to endure Margo's knowing smile. Then, intercepting Boyd, they made their way back to the hall, where the meal was well underway. "If you care to stay?" she asked, indicating his men who were seated among her people.

"I would continue the tour instead, unless you wish to remain."

Before he finished talking, Galia had begun walking once again. She spoke to many in the hall, and then took Boyd from building to building. Introducing him, reassuring all those to whom she spoke.

By the time they'd finished, Galia had one more idea.

"Before I meet with Alan," she said, "there is another place I would show you."

Until now, she'd avoided remembering his embrace, his hand on her cheek. Boyd in that tub, a vision Galia didn't think she could ever truly forget. But now, as the time for them to part once again grew close, she found herself wishing to remain by his side a bit longer.

"This way."

She led Boyd to the charter room at the base of the tower in which he stayed. There, the door was half his size. Galia pulled a wall torch from its base and handed it to him. "If you will hold this."

He took it without question. Then, pulling the ring of keys from her belt, Galia found the small one she looked for. Opening the nondescript wooden door, she pushed it open.

"Have you heard of the monster of Gurstelle?"

"That an English captive has been hidden away for

centuries here?" he asked. Boyd's face lit up from the flame in this darkened corridor. One she rarely visited alone even knowing the myth was nothing more than that.

"Aye. My grandfather refused to be shown this room for fear of a story he knew not to be true," she said, ducking inside the door. Then, reaching out, Galia took the torch from Boyd so he could do the same.

When he did come through, she held the torch up for him to see. "A secret chamber," she said, "housing naught more than a chest and some old tapestries."

Though Boyd could stand upright, he did so with the ceiling not far from the top of his head. The chamber's walls curved inward, the space larger than one might believe from the size of the door but not so large that much more furniture could be brought inside.

"What is this place?"

She smiled. "Where the captive has been hidden," she said. "Of course, there was never one in here, and none are certain where the story began. But this chamber is not known outside Gurstelle's walls. Its people believe the legend staves off some who might otherwise be emboldened to attack us."

"You do not know how the story began?"

"I do not. But when you hear of the captive who takes on a monstrous form in the eve, 'tis here that he resides."

Boyd moved toward her. He reached out, Galia's breath catching once again, but 'twas simply to take the torch from her. "You assume the captive, the monster, is a man?"

Boyd placed the torch in its holder on the wall and came back to her.

"'Tis not I who made that assumption, but indeed, if there were a monster haunting Gurstelle, likely he would be a man."

He took another step toward her. "You believe it to be so?"

She swallowed thickly. "I do," Galia managed.

"Why?"

Another step. He was so close now, Galia could reach out and touch his chest.

"Men are more easily corrupted."

He closed the remaining space. "You've not met the right men if you believe it to be so, Galia."

It was the use of her familiar name, as much as his proximity, that told Galia what was to happen next. He would kiss her, and she'd gladly allow it.

"I've a high regard for some men," she said, her voice soft. "Like Alan. But there are others . . ."

She trailed off as his finger lifted. Boyd placed it on her lips.

"I am not most men," he said, his hand shifting positions so that he now held her chin. Without a word, he guided her to him. Lifted her chin upward as he bent down, his intent clear.

Galia's heart pounded, the anticipation of Boyd's kiss becoming almost unbearable.

When his head lowered, his face so close to hers she could feel his breath, he said, "I would kiss you, Lady Galia of Gurstelle, if you'd allow it."

Her lips parted.

CHAPTER 13

BOYD'S INSTINCTS had never led him astray. He'd been taught to trust them. Taught they could save his life. And yet, they seemed to be abandoning him now, because his instincts toward Galia told him the impossible.

That he belonged with her.

A ridiculous notion if there ever was one. And yet, he did not wish to kiss her for his own pleasure alone. Boyd wished to show Galia that she was wrong. That not all men were corrupt. Or weak, as her father had apparently been. That some, like him, would cherish a woman like her until the end of their days.

Not that he would have the opportunity.

They could never be together, of course. He would not abandon Wallace's cause, and she would never abandon Gurstelle. Even so, he could not resist just one taste of her.

She did not answer him, not in words, at least. But Galia's lips did part, her eyes now staring at his lips. Boyd descended even farther toward her until, at last, their lips touched. He could sense immediately this was a new sensation for her, so he moved slowly.

He pressed his lips to hers, avoiding groaning aloud at the simple pleasure of it. Not wishing to alarm her, but unable to resist, he let his tongue glide across the crease of her lips. With more pressure, he did it again.

She opened for him.

When she did, Boyd took advantage. His tongue sought hers. Tentative at first, but with his guidance, eventually she understood. Boyd released her chin, using his arms to pull Galia into him. Responding by bracing herself against his shoulders with her hands, she deepened the kiss.

The sign he'd been waiting for.

Boyd slanted into her, his tongue no longer hesitant. Increasingly, she understood, as their tongues tangled. As Boyd's hand lowered and pulled her in even closer. Hard, ready for her, but knowing he'd have no relief for it anytime soon, Boyd ignored his body's signs and instead taught her how and where to move.

Soon, the kiss began to spiral. He broke it off, needing more. Boyd pushed her hair back, kissing every bit of exposed skin he could find. The flesh behind her ear. Her neck. Galia made a sound deep in her throat as he kissed lower and lower until his lips found the cleavage he'd tried hard to ignore.

Her rapid breathing teased his ears. Galia's passionate response to him was not surprising even for one so innocent as she. This was a daring woman who would not be cowed by kisses alone.

When he pulled his head up and looked at her, a defiant, even triumphant countess stared back at him. Without words, he pulled her in for another kiss, this one as if it were unleashed from the deep recesses of the secret chamber in which they stood.

By the time they broke the kiss again, both he and Galia

breathed heavily. The air was warm and almost stifling around them.

He did not want to be parted from her, but neither did Boyd think Galia should lose her virginity on this dusty chamber floor.

"You've not been kissed very often."

She shook her head. "Nay. I've not."

"How is such a thing possible? Surely many have tried?"

"A few," she admitted. "But I thought not to chance . . ." She hesitated. "Liking it. Knowing I could do naught about it. So most of them, I simply rebuffed."

"Men have the advantage," he admitted. "In this way."

"In many ways," she said, her lips still swollen from his kiss.

"But in this, for certain."

"Aye," Galia said, staring at him as if in wonder.

"Was it not what you expected?"

"Nay," she said. "It was so much more."

If Boyd were not careful, he would lose his heart to this one. "I am glad to hear it," he said, attempting to lighten the mood between them. Not able to recall a time he wished to make love to a woman more than Galia, he needed some space. A kiss was quite a bit different from what he now envisioned.

A vision he'd do well to dispatch. Boyd was no defiler of virgins. Certainly not a countess such as Lady Galia.

"I am glad to hear it," he said. "And honored you allowed me to be your first."

"I kissed two men before," she said. "Neither used . . . neither did that to me."

A lightness in his chest spread to every part of him. "Then they did not kiss you in truth," he said, refusing to be glad for it. "Any man who put his lips to yours without tasting you as I did is not a man at all. So those I would discount completely. Better to rid your mind of them."

She laughed. "I will do so, sir, as easily as you could do the same."

"Every memory of a woman that came before you is now gone." Terrifyingly, it was true. All, of course, but one. A memory he could neither forget, nor forgive.

"And I thought you to be truthful to me," she said.

Though he was, mostly, Boyd could not dishonor her with even a partial lie. "All but one," he admitted. "A woman I'd thought to marry."

A shadow so briefly crossed her face that Boyd rushed to explain. "The memory I cling to is not one of affection but betrayal. She was with another man. Told me herself, for which I am grateful. It would not have done to marry and then learn of the betrayal."

Her expression, of genuine sorrow for him, tugged more at Boyd's heart than he'd have wished for.

"I am sorry for it," she said. "Any woman who had your love and so wasted it is a fool indeed. You should be glad to have learned of her weak character in time."

Her quick defense of him, the compliment he did not ask for, affected Boyd more than he was comfortable admitting.

"I was glad not to have married her, very much so." He moved toward the wall. "Shall we go? MacCabe will be wanting to speak to you."

As if embarrassed she'd so forgotten herself, Galia lifted her skirts and rushed ahead of him to leave. Boyd stopped her.

"Galia."

She paused and turned.

"Do not let the love you bear for your people make you

forget to be loved yourself. You've a right to it as well as they do."

She thought on his words and apparently dismissed them. "Aye," Galia said, though she did not mean it. She lived for them. Cared for them. Fought for them.

Who, he wondered, did the same for her?

Indeed, all adored her. She counted her maid, her marshal, and even Gurstelle's cook as her friends and confidants. But this was a woman, he thought as they exited the chamber, with no parents nor siblings to speak of. A woman who showed incredible strength despite it.

He wanted to reach out for her. Kiss her once again. Emphasize his words and make her see that she was as worthy as the people she so adored.

Instead, he followed from the dark corridor into the light.

Into, it seemed, utter chaos.

CHAPTER 14

"What has happened?" Galia said as she and Boyd stepped into a lighted corridor.

"Mistress Beatrice, my lady," a maid called as she ran past.

"Something is amiss with her babe?" She did not wait for an answer but made her way toward the tower where all castle officers and their families had chambers, including Beatrice.

"Aye, my lady," said the spicer, a man who'd served Gurstelle for many years. "The babe is coming but Beatrice is bleeding too much. Methinks the babe has not survived."

"No," Galia gasped. It could not be. Beatrice had lost two others, and her desperation to birth a healthy child was well-known to all. None were as caring to the wee ones at Gurstelle, no maid as beloved among the servants as the steward's lovely daughter.

It was only as they reached the corridor outside her chamber, the crowd that had gathered a testament to how beloved Beatrice was, that she realized Boyd was still with her.

His look of concern for a woman he did not know warmed her heart. There was a wildness about his gaze that had Galia reaching for him. The spell seemed to break as he realized her hand lay on his arm. But she'd not been imagining it. There was something there. Turning from him, she broke through the crowd as murmurs of "Lady Galia" created a path for her. When she pushed the wooden doors open, a stench of blood reached her nose.

The midwife knelt beside Beatrice as two others prepared what Galia assumed was the babe. The loss cut as deeply as if it were her own. Tears sprung to her eyes as she realized two things at once.

The swaddled babe was crying and Beatrice was still bleeding.

"More rags," the midwife called. Galia fetched them as she bid and then sat beside the new mother. Her eyes wide, Beatrice asked for her daughter. Apparently, the babe was a girl. Galia's gaze flew to the midwife, who shook her head.

She was attempting to save Beatrice's life.

Galia took one of the rags and wiped Beatrice's brow. With her other hand, she found and grasped Beatrice's and held on tight, murmuring words of comfort.

"I am massaging the womb to stop her bleeding," the midwife said. Though her soothing words were said so calmly that only a woman who'd been bringing babes into the world for many years could manage them, Galia saw the truth of it in the woman's eyes.

They were losing Beatrice.

"I will fetch your daughter," Galia said, still squeezing her hand. "First tell me, what name will she be called?"

Beatrice held Galia's gaze, her eyes clear and true. "Galia, if it pleases you, my lady. I know none more worthy."

Her chest squeezed. "It pleases me very much," she said, attempting to give her comfort. Though she didn't want to focus on the midwife's work, Galia could not resist looking down. Was it wishful thinking, or had the bleeding stopped?

"More hot water," she called as three other servants attended her. "Lift her legs a bit," she added. And the next time she looked, the coverlet was no longer covered in blood, replaced with clean linens. The women began to wash Beatrice's legs.

"The pain is too much to bear," Beatrice said to her.

Galia spoke firmly when she replied. "'Tis not," she said. "Because your daughter awaits." She motioned for the babe to be brought after a quick nod from the midwife affirmed it and ordered one of the serving girls to find a wet nurse.

As Beatrice's daughter was handed to her, the woman seemed to forget her pain. She cried, held her, and offered her thanks to the weary-looking midwife, who Galia knew they didn't deserve. She'd served the Scottish king once and was as skilled as any.

Under another's care, Beatrice would surely have died.

With a kiss on the beautiful babe's forehead, and another for her mother, Galia whispered her thanks for such an honor and left them both in the very capable hands of the others. The midwife met her at the foot of the bed.

"She will be well?"

"Aye, though she cannot feed the babe herself."

"What happened?" Galia whispered.

"A vessel opened when the afterbirth detached. She would have bled out if it continued much longer."

"How did you stop it?" she asked, knowing such an

occurrence may happen again and wanting to understand its solution.

"By ensuring all parts of the afterbirth were removed and continuing to massage the womb. There was nothing else that could be done," she said, looking fondly at mother and babe.

Galia brought the midwife toward her, squeezing and pouring her thanks into her as best she could. "You did more than enough. Thank you," she said.

"'Tis my duty." The midwife suddenly cried out to one of the serving girls. "Nay, do not move her so." Hurrying to the bedside, she began to give the girls instructions. As they covered Beatrice with fresh linens, the midwife went back to work.

Making her way to the door, Galia opened it, found her steward and the babe's father standing next to him, and smiled. "You may go inside. Mother and babe are well. Congratulations on your wee daughter," she said.

The gathered crowd cheered.

"What name has Gurstelle's new babe?" someone asked behind her as she reunited with Boyd.

"A fine name," she answered. "The mother will announce it in her own time."

Boyd looked down at her gown, which was covered in blood.

Their eyes met.

She pulled him away from the others. When they were far enough down the corridor that none could hear, Galia answered the silent question.

"We nearly lost the mother," she said. "Only the skill of our midwife saved her."

"And the babe?" he asked.

"Is well." Galia stopped. "Tell me," she said, thinking of

the way he looked when they'd approached Beatrice's chamber. "There was something in the way you looked at me earlier."

"My mother lost a babe," he said. "A boy. Before I was born."

Her shoulders fell. Naught else was said, but Galia understood the implications of his words. Likely 'twas something that he carried with him if Boyd was the next born after his parents lost their son.

"I am sorry for it," she said, knowing the words were inadequate.

"It seems," Boyd said, his tone lighter, "you are in need of change. Shall I find MacCabe and tell him your meeting will be delayed?"

Galia opened her mouth to say nay. That she could find Alan and meet with him anon. Instead, she reined back the response. She was closer to her own chambers than she was to the solar. Boyd had simply asked an innocent question and would not gloat over her need for him.

"He will likely wish to get back to the defenses. Tell him I give him leave to share an update with you." She smiled. "And if he questions it, as he may, share also that you know his given name was to be Donnchad but changed to Alan the day of his birth."

Boyd's laugh seemed to come from deep within the recess of his stomach. It was a hearty sound, and a pleasing one to her ears. "Donnchad," he repeated. "'Twill be his name to me for as long as I remain here."

A reminder that Boyd would not be remaining long. Days, perhaps.

He seemed to sober as the thought entered her mind. Was he thinking the same?

"If the marshal is not pleased at me for having told you,

relay the news of Beatrice's birth. He holds a special affection for her, as do we all, and will be glad to hear she and the babe do well."

"As you wish, my lady."

His tone was deferential. His bow, not at all mocking. Seeing a man such as him, one of the greatest warriors in the Kingdom of Scotland, most like, and the most skilled swordsman she'd ever see in her lifetime . . . seeing him this way . . .

Galia wanted him to kiss her again.

Nay, she wanted much more than that.

"Tell me why you smile so," he said.

Galia could no sooner wipe the smile from her face than she could imagine what it might be like to make love to a man such as him.

"I will," she promised. "This eve. For now, my bath awaits."

Her cheeks warm from the teasing in her tone, Galia picked up her skirts and walked off in the opposite direction from where Boyd was headed.

The sound he made, a soft but unmistakable groan, echoed throughout the corridor.

Galia's smiled broadened.

CHAPTER 15

He'd not imagined it.

If that kiss were not proof enough, the tone when she'd said, "I will," told Boyd all he needed to know of his growing suspicions that Galia was amenable to his advances. Ones he hadn't wanted to make. Ones he should not make.

And yet ...

"Kerr?" MacCabe obviously had not been expecting him.

Boyd walked into the solar chamber unencumbered. Though guards stood at intervals throughout the keep, none did more than watch him as he strode through. Speaking briefly to his men who trained in the yard, one he intended to return to on the morrow, Boyd closed the door behind him.

"Donnchad," he said, sitting and inviting the marshal to do the same. "'Tis just the two of us."

MacCabe didn't sit. Instead, he seemed to be contemplating how to respond. Finally, Boyd rescued him from his confusion.

"Lady Galia asked that I meet with you in her stead after she attended the steward's daughter's birth."

MacCabe did sit then. "I did hear Mistress Beatrice had some difficulty. She and the babe are well?"

"More than some difficulty," Boyd replied. "The mother nearly bled out, but aye, she is well. The babe too."

"A fitting name for a daughter."

Boyd realized he did not know the babe's name. "What will they call her?"

"Galia," he said. "A tribute to our lady."

Of course Galia hadn't told him that. She was as humble as she was resourceful.

"The countess is much beloved here," he said, though the words hardly needed stating.

"Very much, as was her mother. But Lady Galia has a kindness about her that the late countess did not share. She was not cruel, but neither did she tread lightly on any topic. She was an excellent leader." He sighed. "But as a mother, I fear she was not gentle with my lady."

"Even so, 'tis not difficult to see Lady Galia is gentle with her people."

"Her nature, perhaps? She certainly did not learn as to be so from me, nor Margo, with whom she shares a deep affection."

Curious, then, or perhaps as MacCabe said, 'twas Lady Galia's nature.

"She assumed you would wish to return to the gatehouse," he said as MacCabe shifted uncomfortably in his armor. Boyd himself wore little of it for that reason, being too encumbered, a fact his mother rued every time they met. For her, he wore mail alone, but only in battle.

"Indeed," he said. "The damage is minimal, despite the size of the first boulder. It will take a sennight to repair, and we've managed to set fire to the trebuchet responsible."

"How many others do they have?"

"We are uncertain. But for now, the threat is past. However"—MacCabe frowned—"I fear they are becoming desperate. They show no signs of surrender. Indeed, another patch of woods appears to be dwindling to the northeast."

"Do they use the wood for another sow?"

"Again, we are uncertain. Our only spy in their camp was discovered some days ago."

"Convince her to allow my intervention," Boyd said. She must have known he would use this opportunity to entreat himself to the marshal.

"I am unconvinced Halton will accept your offer."

"Wallace knew his father well from his time in England. He assures me Halton will consider it."

"And free our men to fight with you?"

"Aye."

MacCabe's eyes narrowed. "Tell me of the battle brewing."

The marshal trusted him with information and Boyd would do the same. "It was only because of our own spies that we learned of the impending attack. And could be the biggest blow to Edward since Stirling. We've the king of France's support."

That did manage to surprise the marshal. "Indeed? In what form?"

"Coin. And men. We rendezvoused in this very spot." He indicated the direction from which Boyd and his men came. "In Gurstelle Cove, just before the siege began."

"We? Were you a part of the negotiations?"

"I was."

"I've heard the Brotherhood does not take sides in the succession wars of Scotland but only fights against those who would do harm to anyone who wishes to cross the border safely?"

"And threats to our own family, aye."

"Yet you fight alongside the outlaw?"

Boyd sighed. "My father believes in Wallace's cause. As do I. Others in my family, the Waryns especially, would wish to remain more neutral, but even for them, the time to declare themselves is past. Edward's tentacles grow longer, and stickier, with each passing day."

MacCabe appeared thoughtful. "If you've the French king's support in this battle, why are you here? Surely Gurstelle cannot supply as many men as he."

"True enough," Boyd said. "But he sent fewer than originally agreed upon. And support in the borderlands has waned since Wallace's defeat. I fear Edward's tight grip on the throats of Scottish nobles will be our downfall. A decisive victory against him now might very well bolster the cause we cannot abandon."

"Nay, we cannot," he agreed, thankfully. The marshal stood. "On the morrow, we meet in the training yard. After it, I will see about the support you ask for."

Boyd rose with him, knowing precisely what MacCabe's message was. Defeat him, and he'd consider speaking to Galia on his behalf.

"I await it eagerly," Boyd said. "Your men think highly of your skills as a swordsman."

"With luck they will continue to do so on the morrow. Good day, Kerr," he said. Without preamble, MacCabe left the chamber in the decisive manner in which he did all things.

Boyd remained for a moment, looking through the

chamber in which Galia spent much of her time. Not wishing to intrude any longer on such a private space, he took himself from the solar, intending to return to the men.

Until he thought of their kiss. Of Galia's response to him. She would be bathing now, her attendants likely with her. Boyd could not risk her reputation on a whim, but an idea formed. The maid Ada was married to MacCabe's son. If the marshal learned of what Boyd considered, he would be wroth with him, and for good reason.

If he had more time to consider it, Boyd might have exercised more caution. But on the morrow, he would defeat MacCabe and either convince Galia of his plan or nay. Either way, he could not remain at Gurstelle much longer.

Fully decided, he stopped a serving girl passing by.

"Can you tell me where to find Mistress Ada?" he asked.

The young woman's appreciative gaze, coupled with her silence, forced Boyd to ask more forcefully. "The Mistress Ada?" he repeated.

Her eyes flew back up to his face. "Apologies, my lord. Follow me."

CHAPTER 16

SHE SHOULD BE SEEING to the evening meal. But Galia wished to remain in the tub just a wee bit longer. How long had it been since she'd thought of anything other than the siege? And supplies? And burned crops, or how a physician or midwife might get past Halton's defenses? Today, a life had been saved, but tomorrow, one could be lost. Or more if Halton's bid to snatch Gurstelle from them was successful.

How long had it been since she'd dreamed of a man's kiss?

Not long after her mother passed, an English knight had come to Gurstelle as a guest. His mother Scottish, the man was as handsome as any she'd seen before. He stayed just two nights, his stolen kiss at the back of Gurstelle's stables one she'd welcomed. Like Boyd, he had allowed his tongue to touch her lips, but unlike this time, she had not opened for him. They'd been interrupted by the groom, and Galia had been ashamed of her behavior.

She'd convinced herself the love of those she was responsible for was all the love she needed. Yet Boyd had proven Beatrice correct.

It was not enough.

Though she almost wished the kiss back, as afraid now of knowing what she missed as she'd been before, the memory of it was not something with wish she cared to part.

"Just a moment longer," she said to Ada as the maid opened her door. When she didn't answer, Galia's eyes flew open.

Not Ada at all.

She sank into the tub, submerging her breasts completely. "How is it possible you come to be here?" she asked as Boyd strode through her bedchamber.

The door was locked. A guard, positioned at the entrance to this tower.

"With a bit of aid from Mistress Ada," he said, as if it were the most natural thing in the world to have somehow found himself alone in this chamber with her.

"The guard," she said as he approached.

"Knows nothing. Though you really should speak to the man about his penchant for almond cake. I enjoy it as much as any, but abandoning your post for the sweets?"

She knew exactly of whom Boyd spoke. Resisting a smile, then realizing his intent, Galia's pulse quickened. As she had done exactly, Boyd reached first for the cloth and soap and then for the stool on which both sat.

"Boyd."

He sat behind her.

With the memory of his kiss still in her thoughts, Galia sucked in a breath as his hand dipped into the water at her side. His scent, his very presence behind her . . . and then, his touch. Slowly he brought the cloth up Galia's arm toward her shoulder.

"'Tis only fair I should return your kindness with my own."

When his touch ran across the top of her chest, Boyd switching the cloth from one hand to the other, she sank even deeper. No man had ever seen this much of her, even though just her shoulders and neck, as well as her knees, which were propped up in the tub, were visible.

"I've not heard of this particular custom," she managed.

"Nay? It is quite common where I'm from."

He ran the cloth back again to just beneath her neck.

"You were raised not far from Gurstelle," she reminded him.

His hand slipped downward and paused between her breasts, under the water. Having avoided doing so before, Galia tilted her head back now. A set of clear eyes, trusting and true, stared back at her. When Boyd licked his lips, she was lost.

Nay, she amended silently, she was lost as his hand moved once again. But this time, it held no cloth. When it first touched her nipple, his fingers now splayed over her breast, she almost looked away. But with his free hand, he stopped her. Reaching for her chin, Boyd held her head in place.

"There is nothing shameful," he said, his voice low and seductive, "about finding pleasure." Boyd's thumb and finger teased her nipple. Rolling it between them, he continued. "There is no need to look away."

He dropped her chin but continued to run his hand from one breast to the other.

"We are unwed."

Abruptly, he stopped. Repositioned the stool from behind her to Galia's side.

Without a word, his head dipped toward hers, clearly

dismissing her words. This time, she was prepared. The moment his lips touched hers, she opened for him. Her tongue found his eagerly. What had they been discussing?

Galia could not remember. Not as he kissed her and certainly not as his hand once again dipped inside the water. As flames from the fire found a new piece of wood to burn, a sudden crackling evidence of it, so too did Galia warm to his touch.

His hand explored beneath the surface until it finally slipped between her legs. Though her instinct was to close them, as Boyd's tongue demanded more, she realized he wanted the same from her legs too. Opening them, she was rewarded by a sensation like no other.

He'd slipped his finger slowly inside her. Then, another.

As Boyd's tongue flicked against her own, so too did his fingers, now matching every movement. Advance, and retreat. The pace quickened, as did her breath. It was only when the cold air reached her breasts that Galia realized she was all but sitting up in the tub.

The low moan of pleasure Boyd made, as if he enjoyed this as much as she, had her reaching over to him. Her hand grabbed a fistful of hair as she pulled him even closer. When Boyd's thumb pressed against her, his fingers now circling as if coaxing something from her, Galia nearly jumped from the tub.

Everything was warm now. Her cheeks, her chest, the very air that had been cold just moments ago. It was as if there was something there she could not quite grasp. Until, yes! Just there. She murmured her encouragement even as their kiss continued.

He seemed to understand.

Responding, he shifted his thumb just slightly and . . .

She could hold on no longer. Pulsing beneath the expert

ministrations of his fingers, Galia tightened everywhere. She forgot to continue kissing him as he pulled back, watching her.

"Boyd," she cried as his entire hand cupped her beneath the water. The sight of his smug smile only intensified each and every pulse that seemed as if they'd never end. When they did, she said nothing, for no words could capture how she felt at that moment.

Boyd pulled his hand away, his gaze dipping down to her breasts.

"Galia," he said, making another noise deep in his throat, as if she tortured him.

His eyes rose.

"I did not know," she said simply.

"And now you do." He smiled. "But there's much, much more to learn, my lady."

CHAPTER 17

"Gurstelle has more men than I realized." Ranulf looked up toward the ramparts, pointing out what Boyd knew already.

"Wallace sent us here for a reason," Boyd said, looking for one person in particular, since Galia had not been to the hall to break her fast.

After her maid came to fetch her last eve, Boyd hadn't seen her again. The midwife had summoned her when a wet nurse could not be found. Without being able to leave Gurstelle's walls, this presented a problem not easily solved.

He'd sat with his men, then slept horribly, not having spoken to her since he left her chamber. And now, with the entire castle watching, he would challenge the best swordsman of them all. MacCabe swung his mighty claymore through the air in a way that should not be possible with such a sword. His movements reminded Boyd of his cousin, Holt. A tourney champion known throughout the isle, he would similarly display his skill to an opponent.

It worked on many, but he and Holt had been trained by the same men.

"I've learned he distracts with an overhead strike," David said, "and ends duels with a swift kick to the abdomen."

"If he moves overhead, back away," Robert added. All three men looked at him. "You were advising him just the same," Robert said defensively to David.

"There is a difference between alerting Boyd to his challenger's preferred strategies and telling the greatest swordsman of our time how to fight," David countered.

While the men squabbled, Boyd attempted to clear his mind. He'd been mostly successful until he saw her.

Galia had just come into the training yard with her steward and maid. She sought him out and, spotting him, raised her chin. Boyd could not discern her expression. Was she embarrassed by what had happened between them? Or worried that her maid knew? Did she regret it?

He had no time to ponder the question any longer. Boyd was being called to the center of the yard. The rules of their duel, the same as when he'd faced Gurstelle's other men, were called out. The marshal was a man his father's age, giving him the one thing Boyd lacked—

More experience. Indeed, as their swords clashed and the gathered crowd cheered, everything fell away.

The cold that whipped at his back. His companions. The onlookers.

Even Galia.

As always, he went immediately on the offensive. Boyd would not let up until his opponent's neck was at the tip of his sword, or he was lying on his back. If he did, the hesitation could cost him.

Wallace needed these men. But as importantly—a

disturbing thought Boyd had no time to explore just then—Gurstelle needed to see this siege ended.

MacCabe was good. Very good.

He used every angle available to him. Straight down, straight up. A diagonal strike found its mark, the hilt of Boyd's sword rattling in his hand because of it.

Slowing his breathing, Boyd considered what his father had taught him those many years ago. And sure enough, his companions had been right. Stepping away from what most assuredly would have been a blow that may have surprised Boyd long enough for MacCabe to defeat him, he nearly was able to gain the upper hand.

Instead, both men found their footing once again.

As their swordplay continued at a pace most men would have found difficult to sustain, Boyd contemplated when to make a defining move.

On the morrow, we meet in the training yard. After it, I will see about the support you ask for.

Without this victory, he may not have MacCabe's support. Without that, Galia would prove difficult to convince. She may desire him, but she did not desire to need Boyd's aid.

Now.

Having been able to control the flow of their movements, Boyd swung his sword arm in attack while he stepped right to avoid a counter blow. With every bit of might he could muster, his weapon clanged against MacCabe's as Boyd continued his forward movement.

The force of the blow caused the marshal to stumble backward just enough. Boyd brought the sword edge sideways just below MacCabe's neck. The man actually smiled, raised his right arm in defeat, and waited as the crowd cheered for Boyd's victory.

When the men stepped apart, MacCabe inclining his head to Boyd in deference, more cheers erupted. Boyd found Galia once again, her hand gripping that of her maid. Had she been worried for him? Afraid he might lose?

Or, more likely, that he might win. The choice she had now to make was an obvious one.

"I've defended myself in this yard, and many others. Fought on the battlefield more often than I wish to recount," MacCabe said as both men sheathed their swords. "But never have I encountered a man who fights quite as you do."

As they walked toward the countess, Boyd smiled at one particular memory. "We'd been visiting my family at Kenshire Castle, my father, Reid and my Uncle Geoffrey challenging each other as we've just done. Many were surprised my father bested my uncle, as he was known to be the best swordsman in England for many years. My cousin Holt gets his skill from Uncle Geoffrey. When I asked my father later how he explained his win, he said, "Most master the seven blows of the sword. But it's the four virtues—prudence, celerity, fortitude, and audacity—that will win every duel."

MacCabe was as quiet as Boyd when his father first said as much. But finally, he stopped and asked Boyd a question.

"Which did you employ against me today?"

"Audacity, of course. If I allowed my mind any doubt of my victory against you, the crowd would now be cheering for you instead of me. To think myself a better swordsman than Alan MacCabe borders arrogance."

"And you are not an arrogant man, Kerr."

It wasn't a question, so Boyd didn't answer it. Instead, he bowed to Galia as he and MacCabe finally reached her.

"My victory is, of course"—he stood straight up—"in your name, my lady."

"I thank you for it. And for such a fine display," she said. Then to MacCabe, "Will you walk with me to the wall? We've much to discuss."

"Of course, my lady," the marshal said.

For a moment, Boyd thought he'd been properly dismissed. But just as they made to walk away, her gaze held his.

"As do we, my lord. Will you dine with me in my chambers at midday?"

As the first snowflakes of what appeared to be the beginnings of a late-season snowstorm began to fall, he thought to tell Galia he'd do more than dine with her. But, of course, thought better of saying as much aloud. Instead, he said, "Aye, my lady."

She nodded. "I will send for you. MacCabe?"

Without a backward glance, she was gone. He watched her go as his companions slapped his back, congratulating him on his victory. Boyd was glad for it, but there was another battle he'd not yet won.

And it had nothing to do with Halton, his men, or Boyd's true purpose here at Gurstelle.

CHAPTER 18

"You believe I should allow it?" Galia asked her marshal.

"I do." She and Alan took watch over the blasted white tents that had become as much a part of the landscape as the trees that Halton's men used to create their weapons of destruction.

"You believe the baron will accept?"

Snow continued to fall, the abrupt storm one that could be to their advantage. None knew how much of it would fall, but the more uncomfortable Halton and his men were outside Gurstelle's gate, the better.

"There was a time, my lady, he'd have no choice but to do so. 'If the party to whom the oath has been offered does not wish to receive it,'" he said, as if he repeated the words of another, "'but says that his adversary's pledge of truth can be proven by arms, and the other party will not give up, let permission for combat not be denied.'"

"Whose words are those?"

"King Gundobad," he said deviously.

"A Burgundian king who ruled more than eight

hundred years ago? What weight do his words hold here, in the borderlands, on this day?"

She and Alan spoke often of history. It had been her favorite subject, and the only one Galia anticipated discussing with her tutor when she was a young girl.

"They hold no weight, but the lessons we learn from his siege might be applied to Gurstelle. If Halton is to be victorious, as long as our remaining supply line holds, 'twill be from deceit. I fear many grow restless inside these walls and will become more so when the weather warms in truth."

She feared the same. "Did he not lay siege to his own brother?"

Alan tested her knowledge, and she was glad to remember the tale from her tutor well.

"He did."

"And did not the warlord also kill another of his siblings with a third having gone missing, likely another of Gundobad's victims?"

"He was not a nice man," Alan said, raising his arm in acknowledgement to a guard who waved for the marshal to come to him.

"I should say not," Galia said. "Go to your man. I will think on the matter carefully."

"I see no reason to deny Kerr. He will defeat Halton if the Englishman accepts. Of that, I am certain."

She was as well. "He is a formidable opponent," Galia acknowledged.

"I've encountered none more skilled," Alan said with a quick bow. "With your leave, I will attend to the guards."

"Afterwards, do take your evening meal in my place," she said.

Though Alan's only acknowledgment of her words was

a brief nod of his head, she could read easily his expression of gratitude. It was an honor she'd bestow more often, for him to preside over the meal, but rarely did Galia miss a meal in her hall. For her, 'twas an opportunity to be seen, something her mother advised always. "Be absent," she'd often said, "and your people will begin to question your loyalty to them."

She watched him walk away, Alan's stride swift and sure.

Her mother's had been much the same. Her head always held high. Though Galia didn't remember her father well, she could recall the way he walked, as if he were uncertain of his next destination. It was difficult to miss a father she hardly knew—the time he spent in his solar had been something Galia's mother railed against both when he was alive and even after the coughing sickness took him. It was one of the reasons she advised Galia to be seen, one of many bits of advice she hadn't dared to discard.

But Galia was no fool.

Some of her mother's musings were things she'd been forced to reconsider over the years. Sentiments Galia knew now were born from resentment, being forced to marry a man she cared little for, even knowing 'twas her duty as the daughter of an earl.

As the snow began to fall more quickly than before, Galia looked up to the sky, allowing it to fall on her face. She wished there was someone who could tell her what to do. Should she move forward with her plan to be with Boyd? After what had happened between them, Galia could no longer imagine a life without knowing a man.

And more importantly, did she allow him to fight for Gurstelle?

Galia wiped her face with her hands, the cold wetness

reminding her she was alive. And until Halton broke through those gates, she would remain so. It was her responsibility to keep the people safe, no matter her own feelings. It had become clear the risk of Boyd failing was little. Her hesitation came less from that concern than at the thought that she was not enough. Galia could not do it alone. She couldn't defend Gurstelle when they needed her most.

Instead, Boyd would be their savior.

Knowing now what she had to do, Galia lifted her skirts and made her way carefully down from the ramparts into the courtyard. With each step, warring thoughts assaulted her. Ones of hope. Of dread and disappointment.

And of desire.

Galia had lived for Gurstelle as long as she could remember. And she would continue to do so on the morrow, and with luck, many, many days after it. But tonight, she would not be the Countess of Gurstelle, but instead, simply Galia.

A woman who no longer wished to be denied.

CHAPTER 19

THE MOMENT he stepped into her chamber, Boyd sensed it.

Change hung in the air, which should have had him turning on his heels to return to the hall with his men. He'd left them just moments ago, all three of them, like him, becoming increasingly anxious to have their fate at Gurstelle determined.

Would they retreat from Gurstelle the way they came, with no men and only an appreciation for their lives after having navigated the rocks twice? Or would they leave through the gatehouse, Halton's men returning to England defeated? Either way, they could not remain here for more than a sennight, with or without Gurstelle's men.

He thanked the maid who had let him in. Much shier than her lady, she peeked at him a final time before closing the door. Though he'd been in this chamber before, tonight it seemed transformed somehow. Perhaps it was the thought of a heavier-than-expected snowfall outside making the fire all the more welcoming. Or perhaps it was the lingering of Galia's expression as he pleasured her, the purity of a moment that was seared in his mind forever.

Or the knowledge that he could very well be leaving on the morrow. If Galia did not allow him to challenge Halton, there was no reason for them to remain.

"Ada?" a voice called from behind the dressing screen.

A moment later, she emerged. Galia had never looked lovelier. In a simple deep green kirtle with no adornments, her hair free flowing, she looked less like the Countess of Gurstelle and more just a woman, albeit an extraordinarily beautiful one.

"She failed to announce you," Galia said, gesturing to the table that was set already in the middle of the chamber. Two wooden trays of food, along with a pitcher of wine and goblets, already filled, awaited.

Though it wasn't food or wine that Boyd wanted. But this was no ordinary woman. One did not simply stride into the bedchamber of a countess—even if it was a common meeting space among an inner group of advisors—and take liberties with her.

Except, she did not look at him as if Boyd were just any man. And this, just any meeting.

"Perhaps she did not deem it necessary," he said, wanting to kiss her. Instead, Boyd practiced restraint as her station demanded.

"Clearly, she did not. Will you dine with me?" she asked.

He moved swiftly to pull out her chair.

"I asked for the servants to leave, so thank you," she said, sitting.

Boyd nearly asked, "Why?" but thought better of it. If it was the answer he suspected, certainly he'd not sit comfortably throughout the meal.

"I've spoken with Alan," she said as he poured them both wine.

"A worthy opponent," Boyd said, meaning each word. He had expected as much but was surprised, even so, at the marshal's strength.

"He said the same of you."

Galia picked up a bit of bread and dipped it in a small pot of honey. As she ate, she gave no indication that she had him here for anything more than to discuss Halton. But Boyd knew, as he did his own name, such was not the case.

The air itself crackled between them.

"I would best him, Galia," he said directly.

"Aye," she agreed. "You would."

A victory, of sorts. And yet, there was a hesitation to her speech that Boyd found disconcerting.

"Yet?"

"Yet, so many questions remain."

"Such as?"

"You said 'twould be a fight to the death?"

"Aye, Gal, it would," he said, knowing she'd not like the answer. "Such duels are always so, the stakes too high for anything but."

"You could be killed. Because of me?"

They continued to eat, and drink, as he attempted to reassure her that would not happen. "You admitted that I would best him already."

"And I do believe it to be so. But what if something were to happen? What if . . ." She grappled for a reason. "You were to slip? The ground is wet with snow, and I've seen men stumble in swordplay before."

"I will not stumble," he assured her. "Tell me the real reason you hesitate."

Her chin rose. "That is the reason."

"Fear for my safety?"

"Aye."

"You care so much about my safety, then?"

Her expression softened. "I'd not have an honorable man die for a cause that was not his."

Boyd finished his sip, the wine flowing smoothly down his throat. "The cause is a just one. You are a kinswoman to me now, Galia."

That seemed to surprise her.

"A kinswoman? We've only met but days ago."

"You wound me, my lady. Do you think I am accustomed to risking my life to break through a siege? To losing myself in a kiss such as the one we shared?" He treaded dangerous waters now. "To finding that woman's center within my fingers, watching as she is pleasured for the first time? Surely you realize 'tis not a common occurrence, what we shared."

"Is it not? Men do as much, and more, every day."

"I do not do so lightly, Galia. I can assure you."

"But you don't deny you've bedded women before."

"Nay," Boyd said, putting down the meat in his hand. "I do not deny it. But that fact has little to do with what is between us."

"Our time together is nothing special to you—"

"That," he cut in, stopping her words before they even formed, "is not true."

Galia thought she was one of many. He would dissuade her. "I do not bed women indiscriminately, though I can understand why you might think it." Some of his very own cousins came to mind. "And never have I kissed a woman before and come away from it with as much uncertainty as with the one we shared."

"Uncertainty? About what, precisely?"

She would make him say it, and Boyd would do so

gladly. "I am a warrior, Galia. As you know. A man unprepared for marriage."

"As we've discussed," she responded. "I am also prepared to remain unwed, to protect Gurstelle."

Precisely. It was a fact that should please him. Yet, he found that it did not.

"You are a virgin," he said, stating the obvious.

"I am."

Boyd said what he'd been thinking aloud. There was no other hope for it. "I will not deflower a virgin to abandon her. 'Tis simply not done."

"Deflower? You wound me, Boyd, to think I am as delicate as a flower."

"I think no such thing. But in this, you cannot claim anything but innocence."

"Nay," she agreed, "I cannot. And no longer care to remain so innocent. 'Tis time to shed the girl and become the woman."

"You are no girl. And know it well."

"As you said, on this matter, I am as untried as a squire who never picked up a sword."

"And you wish for me to train you?"

"Aye."

This was for certain the most absurd conversation he'd ever had with a woman. "You would have me take your virginity and then leave Gurstelle, never to see you again?"

"I would."

The thought of being with her was too much to bear. He could not calmly remain seated, so close to her, knowing now what she asked of him . . .

He would show her what a dangerous request it was. One she should not make to any man. Boyd wasn't gentle. He strode to her chair, pulled it out, and did what he'd wanted to do from the moment Gal stepped out from that screen. She offered so little resistance as he helped her stand, that Boyd nearly came undone at the memory of words she'd spoken only moments ago.

You would have me take your virginity?

I would.

He might not be willing to take that from her, but Boyd would certainly take something else, something that could be perilous to hold onto in Galia's position.

He would take her innocence.

CHAPTER 20

HER ADMISSION HAD MADE him angry.

It was the first time she'd seen Boyd truly angry, despite having watched him spar with so many men in the training yard. With them, he was measured. Methodical. Speaking of Halton, Boyd became irritated.

But for some reason, after she'd gathered the courage to admit she wanted to be with him, Boyd was unleashing a punishment she didn't deserve. As he pulled her to standing, though, Galia did not resist. He crushed her into his arms, something she'd wanted since the moment he stepped into the chamber.

When their lips crashed together, it was like their other kisses.

Yet, it wasn't.

His tongue slashed through hers, Boyd's head dipping in a way that bound them even closer. His arms encircled hers as if he never intended to let them go. Their bodies were so tightly pressed together, she could feel him against her, even through her kirtle.

And Galia wanted to feel more.

She tightened her arms around him, pressing her hips to his. In response, Boyd's low moan, coupled with his slow circles, had Galia feeling as if someone had just tossed a pile of dry logs on the fire, turning it from a smolder to an inferno. But the heat had nothing to do with her chamber's hearth and everything to do with the man who consumed her now.

"Dammit, Galia," he said, abruptly breaking their kiss. "Do you understand what you said to me?"

He pulled away completely, and with a sound very much like a frustrated animal's growl, he turned his back to her and walked to the fire. She watched him run his hands through his hair. Watched as Boyd's shoulders flexed through the linen shirt, no tunic to speak of. His backside fully visible, he was as intimidating a figure as ever.

When he turned, Boyd caught her looking.

She pulled her chin up, pretending she'd not been staring at his buttocks. "You are angry with me."

He exhaled a deep breath. "I am angry you would have me take your virginity and leave. Never to see you again."

Of all the things she expected him to respond with, that was not one of them. "You . . . would wish to see me again?"

Any hope, even one she didn't know she had, was dashed when he shook his head. "I would wish for you to be with a man who *could* stay."

Clearly, Boyd was not that man. Not that she expected him to be.

He pursed his lips together. Boyd's eyes flashed as he stared at her mouth. He wanted to kiss her again, but restrained himself.

"You do not wish to marry," she said bluntly, "but take your pleasures anyway. Yet you're angry with me for wanting the same?"

His jaw flexed, but Boyd said nothing.

"I do not wish to die a virgin," she said finally, unable to believe she said such a thing aloud.

His shoulders rose and fell. The flare of his nose should not have made him more attractive. In fact, the man looked downright menacing. Even angrier than before.

But she was not scared.

"If you tell me I need a husband, I will remind you that my mother ruled Gurstelle for many years without one."

"Yet you've hundreds of men outside your walls now."

Every affection she may have had toward him, a more considerable amount than she should want, fled in that instant. To remind her of such a thing! That without him, her cause may be lost.

"Get out."

He looked, for a moment, as if he'd not do as she bid. Instead, Boyd strode to the door, reaching it with such few strides that she didn't even have a spare moment to mourn the loss of what had been between them.

Whipping it open, a feat for how heavy it was, Boyd moved to step through it. Galia was only too happy to close the door behind him, but as she reached him, their eyes locked.

She wasn't certain what he saw in hers, but the inkling of regret, of sorrow, in his was her undoing. Aye, Galia was angry. At herself. At her weaknesses. And certainly, with Boyd.

He was wrong to have said it. But perhaps his words had a ring of truth to them. Torn between wanting to shove him through the door and wanting to pull him inside with her, Galia did neither.

Until the choice was taken from her.

He slammed the door shut and pulled her into his arms.

Their mouths clashed together once again. Boyd's fingers moved quickly and deftly to the ties at her back. When he pushed the kirtle past her shoulders, letting it fall, Galia stepped back, away from the discarded garment. As she did, Boyd removed his shirt. The marks all over his body should not have been surprising to her. He was a warrior, after all, and trained like a man attempting to prove his worth to the world.

She touched one, and then another. He groaned, pulling her toward him again. As her fingers explored, Boyd kissed her, his hands moving to both breasts. His thumbs circled the nipples through her shift, and even with the layer of cloth between them, she could easily feel them peak.

It wasn't until Boyd's hand moved to her cheeks, cupping them so tenderly, at odds with the frantic pace of their kiss, that Galia truly became impatient to learn what it was to love a man. Boyd's hands dropped. They moved to her shift, pulling it off in one swift motion.

"Do not hide yourself," he said as Galia attempted to do just that. The sole time she'd ever been nude before a man was in this chamber with him. But then, she'd had the water to shield her.

"'Tis easy enough to say as you stand before me, half clothed."

More quickly than she thought possible, Boyd removed his boots. And then every other piece of clothing until he too stood nude. "Remedied."

She could not help but stare. Surely that was not made to be inside her.

"Even now, I would talk you from this plan," he said, but she stopped him.

"Though I'm still angry with you, I'd not be swayed."

"Still angry, are you?" he asked, now stalking Galia as if

she were his prey. She moved from the door to the bed, its canopies open as if welcoming them.

"Aye," she said. "Furious."

He lifted her easily beneath the arms, placing her on the edge of the bed. She typically climbed onto it with a stool, but none were necessary this eve.

"I am angry as well," he said, opening her legs, which draped over the side of the bed.

Then he did something Galia didn't expect.

"Why are you kneeling?"

"Lie back."

Why she should obey him, Galia was uncertain. But she did. At least, partly. Too curious not to prop herself on her elbows, she nearly jolted back up as he held her legs open and came toward her.

"Boyd." She attempted to sit up, realizing his intent. But at his expression, Boyd's eyes demanding she halt, his jaw set as if he were going into battle, again Galia did the one thing she swore never to do with a man.

Giving him control over her, she once again obeyed.

At the first touch of his tongue, she wondered why Ada had not mentioned this possibility to her before. At the second, she considered sitting up despite his insistence she do otherwise. 'Twas such a strange notion, for him to kiss her there.

But then his hands pushed her legs wider, forcing Galia back down onto her elbows. Boyd licked her, for no other words could describe it in her head. His tongue circled and flicked, driving sensations up through her body that Galia hadn't known were possible.

When he moaned with pleasure, as if it were he and not she that were the recipient of such a scandalous thing as this, Galia gripped the coverlet in her fists. The same building inside her belly, as if she couldn't breathe easily, that she'd experienced in the tub, coursed through her.

Her body tensed everywhere, but it was looking down at Boyd, seeing him kneeling between her legs as he did, that pushed her over whatever edge she'd been teetering on until now. She called out his name, knowing none could hear her but also not caring if they did. Before she could truly recover, he was there. Pushing her atop the bed.

Above her.

She grabbed his arms, so large and muscled that they did not make it easy to hold on to. Galia attempted to catch her breath but could not.

"Are you certain of this?" he asked, his voice low and gruff, as if he were still angry. But his expression said otherwise. It was full of an emotion Galia could not name.

"I am certain," she said with the same surety as if she sent her men into battle. The stakes were not as high, of course, but the feeling, similar. The decision had been made, and she'd not look back from it.

Boyd reached down between them, and she braced for it. Having seen him, Galia was unconvinced this would work. He eased himself into her, the fullness of it like nothing she could compare it to.

He stopped. "Your virgin's barrier," he said.

Galia did not hesitate. "Is yours."

As Boyd's lips met hers, he pushed upward. The pain, though expected, did not abate simply because she willed it to be so. Thinking instead of his kiss, of Boyd's tongue and how it made her feel, it finally began to diminish.

Boyd moved. Slowly, at first, as if he'd break her. But eventually, with her encouragement, more quickly. He circled her, as they'd done earlier, but now there were no clothes between them. Indeed, she and Boyd were joined as one.

No longer in any pain, Galia met his thrusts with her own. Pushing and circling her hips as he did, Boyd's bare chest touching hers, his kiss, his backside, which she now explored with her hands. All of it, together . . . that glorious feeling built again.

"Boyd," she panted as he lifted her again. "Please."

He seemed to understand. Suddenly, his hand was there, his thumb pressing down upon her as if he knew precisely how to make her feel the same as before.

"Come for me, Gal. Find your pleasure with me inside you."

His words. His touch. Galia could not hold on, nor did she wish to.

With a final squeeze of her hands, she called his name again. Boyd entered her so fully, just one last time, and then pulled from her. It was a moment later, after she regained her breath, that she realized he'd moved from atop her. Boyd had taken himself in hand, and as she looked down to see a cloth around him, one she hadn't realized he'd even brought into bed, Gal remembered to be mortified.

"I forgot," she said, "to ask for you to stop at that moment. I'd have . . ."

She'd have allowed him to spill his seed in her. How could Galia have been so irresponsible?

Boyd jumped up from the bed. "Your thoughts were otherwise occupied," he said as he moved to the bowl of water ever present near her bed. He took another cloth from beside it, wet it, and came back to her.

Galia expected him to hand it to her. Instead, he knelt before her once again. This time, for an entirely different purpose. And as he wiped the blood from her legs, as tenderly as he was savage earlier, Galia's chest constricted.

But she could not care for him, not in that way. She refused to be so foolish.

"No longer a virgin," she mused aloud.

"It should not have happened."

Again, she propped herself on the bed by her elbows. "I would not have the only man I've been with regret it."

"I regret only that I took from you what your husband should have. But I could never, ever, regret what happened between us, Galia. That it shouldn't have happened does not change that I am glad it did."

She smiled, remembered she was angry at him, and frowned instead.

"As am I. Even if I'm still wroth with you for reminding me of my failure with Halton."

Boyd climbed into the bed. Pulling the coverlet down, he scooped Galia into his arms and covered them both. With the candles flickering next to them, the fire needing more wood but still burning, he apologized for the remark.

"I should not have said it, knowing you would mistake my words. I meant only that all people must rely on others at times, and you are under siege."

Galia said nothing. Instead, she allowed her head to fall in the crook of his arm. They were silent for some time, Galia content to feel the gentle pull of her hair as Boyd twisted it in his fingers, dropped it, and began anew.

"Let me help you, Gal. Let me fight for Gurstelle. For you."

CHAPTER 21

"OPEN THE GATES."

Though he'd say nothing, Boyd stood beside Galia and MacCabe as they waited for Halton's man. The gears creaked while they stood at the entrance of the gatehouse in Gurstelle's outer ward. Though they could not see the portcullis from here, the menacing sound of its opening underscored their purpose.

Boyd would end this siege, relieve Galia from Halton's clutches, and bring her men to defeat Edward. He needed only for the Englishman to agree.

"Bloody bastards," David muttered next to him. The other men, and Galia's men-at-arms, stood behind them. As the inner portcullis rose, they spotted Halton's banners for the first time.

Boyd glanced at Galia.

Chin raised, head held high, the countess stood next to him. Very different from the passionate woman who he'd held in his arms after their lovemaking. This was a woman who taunted her enemy into making mistakes. Who was as fearless as any person Boyd knew.

He couldn't resist the upward tug of his lips that was certain to infuriate Halton's envoy. It did, though he'd not been trying to goad the man. No matter; let his feathers ruffle, as it were. His master would be dead soon enough.

"Your swords," MacCabe called to the three men, all of whom wordlessly handed them over.

"We come," said the man in the middle, "at the behest of Lord Halton by request of the countess of Gurstelle. What are your terms of surrender?"

Boyd hadn't meant to chuckle. Of course, all three of Halton's men looked at him. He deferred to Galia, a vision in white like the freshly fallen snow. "There is to be no surrender," she said. "My flags were simply to ask you here to propose terms."

All three men stared at her, and then each other, in confusion. "Terms? What terms?" Halton's man demanded.

Boyd and MacCabe stepped forward in sync at his tone.

He waited for Galia to give him leave to speak. When she nodded, Boyd answered. "I would challenge Lord Halton to a judicial duel to end this siege, by the precedent set forth by your own King William the First."

Clearly, they'd not been expecting those words.

"Gurstelle's champion is you?" the smaller of the two men said, with a crowd of onlookers now gathered. "And not the marshal?"

When all three men turned to MacCabe, the marshal said nothing. Galia responded instead.

"My champion is Boyd Kerr of Clan Kerr, son of Reid and nephew to the clan's chief."

They'd agreed naming him might aid their cause. Surely Halton could not resist fighting one of the very men that his own king railed against for their clan's "collusion" with the outlaw William Wallace.

It seemed to have worked.

No longer did the Englishman appear amused.

"My terms are these." Galia looked straight at their leader, her expression as fierce as a lioness protecting her cubs. "A judicial duel will be fought in this very spot with no more than five present on either side. If Kerr is victorious, you will leave Gurstelle land immediately. If the baron . . ." Her voice did slip then. "If the baron is victorious, you will allow all those who wish to leave safe passage before claiming this keep."

Knowing how difficult those words were for her to speak, Boyd marveled at the strength of her voice in doing so. As if she'd not shed a tear last night even discussing the possibility of Boyd's defeat. As if she were not putting the fate of her birthright in his hands.

Boyd did not waver in his belief that Halton would be defeated, but he knew Galia, even though she'd seen him fight, could not be as certain as he.

None said a word. A horse neighed in the distance, but no other sound could be heard. No children laughing or voices being carried through the courtyard as Gurstelle prepared for the midday meal.

Silence stretched.

Until finally, their leader blurted, "I will bring your terms to my lord." With no indication of their thinking on the matter, all three turned and left, as swiftly as they came. Each were handed back their weapons, a moment tense with possibilities. Negotiations to end sieges were often fraught with worries of an attack or other nefarious dealings. But this one, at least, ended peacefully. The men were allowed to leave with their swords hanging by their sides.

As the portcullis closed, those who remained turned to each other.

MacCabe expelled a breath, looking upward to the ramparts, where archers relaxed their stances and all slowly returned to normal. "Patrol, ale," he said. "Unfortunately in that order. The rest is up to him," MacCabe said with a slight bow to Galia. "My lady, leave to see the men far from our walls?"

"Of course," she said, MacCabe already leaving them at her response.

For the first time since they'd stepped from the keep, Galia met Boyd's eyes. A vulnerability none would likely even notice strengthened his resolve.

"He will accept your terms," Boyd said, attempting to reassure her.

Galia frowned, lifting her skirts. "That is precisely what I fear most."

SHE SHOULD HAVE GONE BACK into the hall, but as Boyd followed MacCabe to the gatehouse, his men to the training yard with her own, Galia was not ready to return. To oversee the meal. To assure those she met along the way that all would be well.

In truth, she did not know if it was so.

Instead, she pulled her mantle tight and made her way to the same ramparts where she'd been staring out at Halton's bloody tents for so many days.

She'd made the right decision.

It mattered little that Galia had not wanted to put Gurstelle's fate in the hands of another. A man, and not one she'd known and trusted her entire life, like Alan. Giving him the care of Gurstelle's men-at-arms was never something she struggled to do. 'Twas obvious she could not train or lead her men, even if she wished it otherwise.

But Boyd was not Alan. He was precisely what her mother had railed against. How often had she warned Galia a husband would care little for her thoughts? She would either marry someone like her own father, who cared more for ale than he did for his legacy and people, or marry just the opposite. A man like her uncle, also now deceased, who'd attempted to take Gurstelle from Galia's mother when her husband passed. A man whose ambition was matched only by his miscalculation of women. Specifically, Galia's mother.

I gave myself to him.

And in truth, Galia would do so again. Boyd was everything, and more, she could have hoped for in a first lover. He cared more for her pleasure than his own, and gave it to her freely. She'd been defenseless against his plea to aid her, and knew this siege had to end. Soon.

So they'd sent word. And now the duel had been offered. The baron's acceptance, uncertain. If only there were someone to tell her if she'd made the right decision.

Galia could ask for advice from Margo or Ada about Boyd the man, or ask Alan about Boyd the warrior, but there was just one person who could put together all of the pieces that were Gurstelle's puzzle. And that person was her.

"Do you wish to be alone?"

She had not heard him come, but at the sound of Boyd's voice, Galia spun toward the courtyard, away from the ominous scene before her.

"I did," she admitted. "Until now."

Rewarded for her honesty with a smile, one that would have Galia offering her virginity all over again were such a thing possible, she welcomed him with one of her own.

Boyd stood beside her, Galia looking back out to the sea of tents.

"I would kiss you if the guards were not so close," he said, the wind howling at their backs.

She glanced at a guard, far enough away he could not hear their voices but, as Boyd said, close enough to see their movements.

"I fear between Ada and Margo both knowing what transpired between us, 'twill not be long before whispers make their way through Gurstelle." Galia looked up at Boyd.

His hand moved from the hilt of his sword to clasp hers, covering their joined hands with the folds of his cloak. "I am sorry for having involved your maid," he said. "Though not sorry enough that I regret touching you in that tub."

His words brought a stirring in Galia's core that she understood better today than she would have before. "'Tis not my maid that concerns me most. I adore Margo, and know she would not spread rumors or even share my secret, but the kitchen maids have a way of pulling information from her once they suspect it."

Though their hands were both gloved, Galia could still feel the strength of Boyd's fingers wrapped around her own.

"Ahh, poor Margo," he said, still smiling.

"You've told me so little of your own home," she said, content to listen to Boyd tell her about his parents and sister. About his clan, and even how he met William Wallace. Though becoming cold, Galia would not have moved from this spot for the world.

"Why do you fight alongside him when some of your

other family members do not?" she asked. Boyd risked much, especially with half of his family being prominent Northumberland lords. Ones who were falling out of grace, it seemed, with the king who granted them the power and land they now held. 'Twas a delicate dance, to be certain.

"We know not where the winds of leadership of our country blow. Clan Kerr hesitates, rightly so, to declare for any one future king. But 'tis certain, Wallace fights for the freedom of a people too long with their necks in King Edward's noose."

"And your cousins?"

Boyd sighed heavily, his hand still firmly gripping hers. "Some do, like my cousins Conall and Galien. Even Rory, a Waryn, and his English brethren do as well. But others can not involve themselves as I do. Breac, for instance, as Lord Warden. Or Blase, a tourney knight, whose parents fear his involvement, worrying he will meet a host that doesn't take kindly to his family colluding with the most wanted man in England."

"How do you reconcile it? Your family's differing opinions on the matter?"

"With arguments aplenty."

"Who do you argue with most?"

"Ach, 'tis easy enough to answer. My Uncle Geoffrey's son Holt. The boy is alone in his claim to having bested me in a duel, and refuses a rematch so I might right the wrong."

"Boy? He is young, then?"

"Has seen just two more than twenty summers."

"Yet he bested . . . you?" Galia had difficulty imagining such a thing.

"All of us, Kerr and Waryn alike, say we would gladly die for those we love. Even the ideals we hold true. But neither do we court death. Holt, however . . . he will get himself killed on the tourney field one day defying death so often. The man is fearless, unnervingly so."

"Is he a boy, or a man? You've named him both."

"'Tis certain, it depends on the day."

"This from a man who has just challenged a renowned swordsman to a judicial duel." The thought of Boyd and Halton engaged in a swordfight turned Galia's stomach.

"We've established I am certain to win, have we not?"

"Aye."

"Then do not look at me," he teased, "as if I am a dead man now walking your ramparts. I can assure you, unlike Holt, I've no desire to die."

"I had wondered . . ."

Boyd turned inward, nearly facing her. "I wish to live. To see my cousins give birth to the next generation of Kerr and Waryn children."

"But not your own?"

He did not answer. Galia thought he'd ignore the question, and he stared so long at her lips she thought he might kiss her in full view of the guards. Indeed, she'd have allowed it.

"I thought to delay my own until a time our country was safe."

"Thought?"

Boyd did not elaborate. Instead, he raised his head back toward the fields in front of them. At first, she thought he simply avoided the question. But as Galia continued to follow his gaze, she saw what he did. A banner moving toward their gates. One man, with a white flag. Another holding nothing, and a third flaunting the coat of arms of Halton's house. They moved closer and closer, both she and Boyd realizing what it meant.

"Our answer," he said, letting go of her hand, "seems to be arriving already."

Unbidden, tears formed in the corner of her eyes. She raised her chin to gaze at him, trying to find any fear that might be hidden in Boyd's eyes. But there was none. Instead, she saw only concern.

For her.

With his gloved thumb, he wiped her eyes.

"Do not worry for me, Galia," he said. "Come, let us hear the baron's response."

She would, but in her heart, Galia knew it already. She'd held the Englishman at her gates for so long, deflected his every move and engaged in siege warfare with the bastard who'd come to claim her land and title. They'd not met, but Galia had a sense of the man and could guess his response.

'Twas why she had hesitated for so long. In her heart, Galia knew.

This was the beginning of the end.

CHAPTER 22

"AGAIN."

Boyd cared little that his opponent wished to stop. Besides MacCabe, he'd found no better swordsman here than his own man. Ranulf had become friends with Wallace when they were just boys, and the two trained together for years. He relied on that training now as Boyd prepared for a fight that would have him lose his head were he not victorious.

In two days' time, he would duel Halton.

He hadn't been surprised by the response. By all accounts, the Englishman was spent. Galia had met his best efforts to take this important borderland holding, and Halton had failed. The snow would not have aided his cause, which was, Boyd felt certain, all but lost.

Trading his life for Gurstelle would be an easy decision. This defeat would not endear Halton to his king, and Boyd was certain the man had full confidence in his ability to best most any other swordsman.

But Boyd was confident in the same.

A flash of bright green caught his eye near the entrance

to the training yard. He'd not seen Galia since yesterday when the baron delivered his answer. Though he had been disappointed when she sent word to the hall that she had retired for the evening, Boyd could not think on that disappointment now.

But he did. And slipped.

The yard gasped as the tip of Ranulf's sword rested against the padded gambeson of Boyd's chest. Even his opponent seemed surprised to see it there. Boyd's sword arm froze. He lifted it, finally, in defeat.

"Again," he said, but Ranulf was not listening to him.

"Let another take my place," he said, stepping back as Robert came forward. "I would like to end the day with a victory that I never expected to have nor will be likely to ever see again."

Boyd locked eyes with Galia. She was as surprised as any and appeared properly appalled as well. If Ranulf were Halton, he may now be dead.

I've been training all day. There is naught to worry about.

Though he tried to communicate the silent message, Boyd was forced to give his attention back to Robert. Defeating him three times easily, he finally relented. It might be time to quit for the day, as the sun had begun to set. Tomorrow, he would rest again.

His men, and some of the others he trained against, surrounded him.

"You were distracted," Ranulf said, correctly assessing how he'd come to defeat Boyd.

"Aye," he agreed, not looking back at Galia now. The others would notice.

He looked back only later, after he'd broken down the strategies he'd used, as his training partners had come to expect. Boyd was glad to share his knowledge, perhaps as glad as he should be that Galia was gone.

He could not afford that kind of distraction again.

David echoed his thoughts. "Do you remember," he said as the men cleaned their swords and the others dispersed, "the day . . ."

He stopped.

Ranulf and Robert waited for David to finish, but he said nothing.

Which is when it occurred to Boyd what story his clansman had planned to tell. Not willing to allow Marian to have any power over him, Boyd did it instead.

"I beat my father for the first time. All in the training yard cheered; the woman I . . ." He would not say loved. If he had loved her, and Boyd was unsure of the fact now, he still had little desire to remember her as the object of his affection. "Had grown close to calling my name."

"As you were engaged in training?" Ranulf asked, perplexed.

"Indeed."

All were properly appalled.

"Though Boyd had defeated his father, he quickly found himself on his back for the distraction," David said.

"The lesson . . ." Boyd remembered it well. "Unless your opponent is dead or severely injured, do not count him out. Do not celebrate too soon."

"A good lesson." Ranulf smiled. "But I will take my victory today nonetheless."

"One well deserved," Boyd said, trying not to allow the setback to worry him. Nor would he allow the memory of Marian to bother him.

Galia is not Marian.

It was a true enough sentiment, but the reminder of a

woman that had so wronged him had come at a time when he needed it most. At a time when he'd begun to think of Galia in ways that were too dangerous to contemplate.

Standing with her yesterday, hand in hand . . .

Galia in the tub . . .

Their lovemaking . . .

He must cease such thoughts. Boyd was here for the countess's men, not, he reminded himself, for the countess. He would do well to remember that, lest he get himself killed.

"We celebrate this night," Ranulf said. "To the baron's good sense in accepting his defeat—"

"His death," David added.

"Aye, both," Ranulf continued. "And allowing us to leave Gurstelle from the gatehouse. If I never see those rocks of Gurstelle Cove again . . ."

As they finished with their swords and made their way to the hall, an uneasiness settled in Boyd's stomach. It had naught to do with his defeat today, and everything to do with Galia's absence last eve. That knowledge was a problem, and Boyd had best clear his mind of such notions.

A feat that had just been made more difficult with Galia standing before him.

CHAPTER 23

"I would speak with you," Galia said, despite having waylaid him while Boyd was with his companions. They watched her carefully, likely knowing all that was between them.

"Of course, my lady. Though I fear I am not presentable, having come from the training yard."

He was displeased with her, and Galia did not blame him. Last eve she'd played the coward, hiding in her bedchamber as if she were but a young girl and not the Countess of Gurstelle. Unable to reconcile her feelings for him, she'd retreated. Spent the evening speaking to all whose counsel she respected. Galia had then gone out to the guardhouse to speak with the men closest to the danger that was Halton. Their spirits had been bolstered by the very real possibility of an end to the siege. None seemed worried that Boyd would lose. That Gurstelle could possibly fall into the hands of the Englishman. Rather, the reigning sentiment was that the siege would end soon.

"Would you prefer to meet me at the evening meal instead?"

"Nay," he said without pause. His companions bid them both adieu, and Galia led him to the solar chamber. Like most castles of this size, the solar was fairly large and well-appointed. It was empty, as well.

Galia resisted throwing herself into his arms the moment they walked inside, the fire already having been stoked, wall torches lit. 'Twas what she wanted most to do —Boyd's touch and the feel of his lips were things she'd begun to crave.

But that would not make their parting any easier.

Instead she moved to a chair by the fire, and he did the same.

"I should have asked for wine or ale to be brought," she began, more hesitant than was her custom.

"Why did you avoid me last eve?" Boyd did not mince words or waste time with pleasantries.

What could she say to him? That she'd not expected their night together to have affected her this way? That she wished to be with him again, despite that he would leave Gurstelle with her men in a few short days? She would be precisely the woman Galia had claimed she would not be. Who, after just one eve together, had dreams of them together. Something Boyd would not consider, as she knew well.

Galia had pressed him to take her virginity, and she'd not complicate that action with a bid for more. Something Galia wasn't even sure she herself wanted. Indeed, she'd take no husband. Boyd included.

And yet . . .

"I was with the men," she began, but Boyd cut her off.

"Goddammit, Galia. We spent most of an eve together in each other's arms. I took your womanhood, and you responded by running away from me."

"I ran nowhere," she lied. "I've duties here at Gurstelle, as well you know."

"Duties which prevented you from taking your meal in the hall? Something which your men say is rare, but suddenly necessary? At least offer the truth to me, Galia. You avoided me. Why?"

'Twas futile to deny it. "I know not what to think. And you will be gone," she finished, her argument weak, "very soon."

He waited for her to finish, but she had little more to offer.

"So we will use the time I have remaining pretending that night did not occur? Pretending you did not hold my hand out on those ramparts?"

Of all the things he could have referenced—either of their baths, the way she lay in his arms as they spoke of their childhood, or of course, their lovemaking—why that one?

"I pretend nothing," she said. "You knew when you arrived we were a castle under siege. I am the Countess of Gurstelle," she said, warming to her argument, "and am responsible for its people."

"And I am nothing more than a way to pass the days in the meantime?"

He was becoming more angry, and not less, as they spoke.

"Of course you are more," she said, wondering what he wanted. Boyd was clearly angry she'd avoided him. Was clearly angry now for her weak argument as to the reason. "I suppose," she said, remembering one of the reasons her mother wished for her not to marry, "you wish for us to couple again? Is that why you are so angry?"

A tick in Boyd's jaw was the only indication he'd even

heard her words. Clearly, 'twas the wrong thing to say to him.

"I will duel with a man to free Gurstelle from its siege, and you think that is all I wish from you?"

She would not accept that argument. "You do so for Wallace. Not for me. Not for my people."

"Aye," he said, leaning forward in his chair. "For Scotland," he said quietly. "Lest you forget the reason I've aligned with Wallace in the first place."

"For Scotland then," she conceded. "But do not pretend 'tis for me you are here."

"Very well."

Their eyes locked. Galia would say more. Tell him the reason she avoided him last eve was because she'd grown to care for him too much. If she did, he would laugh his way from the chamber.

"Is that all, my lady? If so, I would rejoin my men. They've been asked to dine with the guardsmen this eve."

"At the gatehouse?" she asked, surprised how quickly her men had accepted not just Boyd, who would fight for Gurstelle, but his companions too.

"Aye," he said, his expression as void of emotion as his tone.

She stood, wishing for more from him, but not receiving it, with aught else to discuss. "You've my leave," she added, hoping for more. Knowing she'd not see him again this eve if he went to the guardhouse. "If you wish it."

He stood as well. Again their eyes locked, and she thought he might take her opening and say more. Tell her that, nay, he did not wish to join his men. That he understood why Galia had not come to the hall last eve—because she was confused, and scared. Her feelings for him were like nothing she'd been forced to reconcile before.

But he didn't, of course.

"Good eve, my lady," he said with a bow.

And then, he was gone. Leaving the chamber without a backward glance. Though Boyd closed the door softly, it sounded to her ears like a thud. Similar to the beat of her heart, heavy with the knowledge that Galia had been attempting to fight against.

She was doing the one thing her mother had advised against above all. The one thing that could "see Gurstelle wrested from you even quicker than an English army."

Galia was considering what it might be like to have a man such as Boyd for a husband.

Even worse than that.

She was actually falling in love with him.

142

CHAPTER 24

BOYD HAD MANAGED to avoid her since they last spoke, but today he could do no such thing. She looked at him now, as they stepped into the courtyard, in a way he had never seen her do before.

Terrified.

For him? For Gurstelle? He could not be certain. Either way, it mattered not. Despite that he'd been so angry when he left her chamber, he had returned to the training yard to take his frustrations out on the wooden pell, he could not ignore such an expression.

Without hesitating, he left the men, strode to her, and said, "Come with me."

Ignoring the stares, he moved to the side of the keep, aware they could still be seen. But from here, at least, they could not be heard.

It seemed all of Gurstelle was in the courtyard now. Since there would be just five of them making their way to the outer bailey where the duel would take place, Boyd assumed they had gathered to watch him part. Which he would do, after speaking to her first.

"You are afraid," he said, having thought of this moment more even than the one he'd face soon. Galia had consumed his thoughts despite her rebuff of him earlier.

"Aye," she admitted. "And like it not."

"I will not let him take Gurstelle," he assured her in a tone that brooked no argument. But instead of being reassured, her eyes widened.

"I fear not for Gurstelle," she said, as if surprised he suggested it. "But for you."

"Me? There is naught to fear for me," he said.

"You faltered." She blinked. "In training. With your man, Ranulf. If that had been Halton . . ."

"I was tired," he said. "And had trained for much of the day by then. This is not training." He gestured to where Halton would meet him. "I will not lose this fight, Gal."

"Do you promise me?"

He would have laughed, except she was not jesting. He knew real fear, had seen it in men's eyes in battle before. She was truly afraid.

For him.

Boyd could say she did not need his promise, that he fully intended to remain alive this day. Instead, wishing to take her in his arms despite these past few days, but knowing he could not with their audience, he forced her to look up directly at him instead.

"I promise you, Gal, I will win this duel. Today is the last day you will see Halton's men at your castle walls."

"You will not die today," she said, as if she had not heard him.

"Nay, I will not."

She was frightened still.

"If I died without bidding adieu to my mother, she would haunt me for all my days. My sister too," he added, thinking of Laire. She risked much as a spy, and understood their fight against the English was a dangerous one, but even still, his sister would not take his death well. Though they saw each other less than ever these past two years, he considered Laire his best friend and would not leave her so abruptly.

"I should not have let you leave," she said, glancing over his shoulder to where the men waited and the crowd, by the sound of it, continued to gather.

He wanted to kiss her. To ask her why, again, she'd avoided him.

Mayhap it was the same reason you did her.

He could have returned to the hall last eve after he'd eaten with the men. Or he could have not gone to the gatehouse to join them at all. Or acted on the impulse to visit her bedchamber, to demand more from her.

But he had done none of those things, because Boyd would be leaving soon, and perhaps 'twas best to sever their ties sooner. Did she think the same? That 'twould be easier this way?

"They call for you," she said. But Gal did not move.

"Aye."

Ask her. Ask her, "Did you avoid me for fear of the hurt it will cause us both when I leave Gurstelle? Do you care for me, Galia?"

He'd presume much to ask such a question.

Instead, he remained silent. Until the calls could not be ignored.

"I must go."

He assumed she would follow, for him and for Gurstelle. But Galia did not move to join him. Cocking his head, he asked the silent question.

She answered. "I cannot watch. I should. But I cannot."

And that's when he knew.

This was the same woman who taunted a powerful English baron from her ramparts. Who led her people through a siege. Who had no parents, no husband, no friends to speak of but those who served her.

Galia did not remain behind because she did not wish to witness a swordfight.

She did so because she loved him.

And God save him, he loved her too.

Neither meant much for anything beyond a sentiment. Her duty was here, with Gurstelle. His was with Wallace. Even if she wanted a husband, which she did not. Or if he wanted a wife, which he did not.

Still, he took that knowledge with him into the courtyard as cheers greeted him. He looked at none but found the marshal, nodding.

'Twas time.

To free Gustelle. To end this siege.

And Halton's life.

CHAPTER 25

"My lady?"

Beatrice was, of course, surprised to see her. All knew the duel would take place at any moment. But as always, the kitchen did not rest. When Galia entered, Beatrice immediately came to her.

"I cannot," Galia said, and Beatrice knew of what she spoke. They rounded the corner, Beatrice wiping her hands on her well-worn apron.

"I've not known you to shy from difficulties before," Margo said, speaking to her as a friend and not as Gurstelle's cook.

"'Tis different." As it had all morn, a vision of Boyd at the end of his man's sword from their training session disturbed her thoughts. Then another, of Boyd lying on the ground. Halton above him, prepared to deal the final blow. Despite that she did not know what the baron looked like, as he'd sent messengers in his stead, Galia could see the scene well in her mind.

"You should be out there," Beatrice echoed Galia's thoughts.

"I know it well. But he could be killed," she said, realizing what that meant for Gurstelle.

What that meant for her.

"He will not. You said it yourself."

"We fought," she admitted.

Beatrice appeared thoughtful. "He was wroth with you?"

"Aye, for avoiding him. 'Twas odd," she admitted. "He said, 'So we will use the time I have remaining pretending that night did not occur? Pretending you did not hold my hand out on those ramparts?'" Galia began to pace the small corridor outside the kitchens that led abovestairs. "Of all that transpired between us, was it not strange for him to mention that particular moment? Of course I did not pretend that night had not occurred. It was I, and not him, who lost my maidenhead that eve."

"Did you avoid him, or nay?"

"Aye, but—"

"Because you fear your growing attachment to him?"

She could admit it easily to Beatrice. "Aye. My mother—"

"Is dead."

Galia met the clear blue eyes framed with as many wrinkles, it seemed, as years Margo had been alive. For a moment, she stared in disbelief at the bluntness of Beatrice's words. But, of course, they were true. Her mother had been dead for many years now. And still she seized control of her thoughts. Of her actions.

"If not for her guidance," Galia defended her mother, "I'd not have been able to rule Gurstelle alone. I would have married and given control of it to my husband."

Beatrice sighed. "Perhaps. The late countess guided you well in many things. But on this matter? Aye, you are here with me in these kitchens because you fear losing Gurstelle to the Englishman, or because you fear for Boyd?"

"Both," she said easily.

"If 'twas another man, and not Boyd, out there. Would you be here, in the kitchens?"

"No," she admitted, just as easily. "I would not."

"A smooth sea does not make a skillful mariner, Galia."

Here, along the coast, the words were common knowledge. That Beatrice should remind her of them now . . .

"I am less afraid of the sea than I am . . ." She stopped. What, precisely, was she afraid of most? The answer came as easily as the others. "He would not control me," she admitted. "Boyd is not such a man."

"So what, then, do you fear?"

"He cannot stay," Galia said. "He fights for Wallace, and has told me plain he wishes not for a wife."

"As you've told him plain the same. 'Tis not a husband you rebel against but the wrong husband."

"He will not stay," Galia said. "Asking him to do as much is futile."

"Watching him ride away for you to wonder what might have been. Asking him to do as much would be foolish, and futile"?

She didn't answer.

Had the duel begun?

She must talk to him again. Reaching for Beatrice, she pulled her close, hugged her, and ran. Lifting her skirts, Galia ran up the stairs, and mindful of the light coating of snow that still remained, she ran through the inner courtyard. Ignoring the strange looks she received as faces whizzed by her, Galia continued to run until she came to the inner gatehouse. Before she reached it, the portcullis was already lifting. Breathing heavily, she willed it to lift more quickly, and ducking under it, ran once more.

Her throat hurt from the cold hitting it as Galia's deep breaths became gulps. The small gathering, as prescribed in Halton's terms, was there already. And Galia's fears come true.

She could say naught to him now. The duel had already begun.

Running to Alan, she stopped just as a loud clang of swords pierced her ears.

"They've begun," she said, standing beside the wall where, not far from them, the exit from Gurstelle Castle led to an army of unwelcome men.

Alan did not answer but simply looked at her. He said naught about her absence, but she wished to address it. "I did not come earlier—"

"I understand, my lady."

Did he? They'd not spoken of her relationship with Boyd, but certainly Alan suspected something between them.

Forcing herself to watch, cursing herself for not having come sooner, it was the sounds that Galia noticed most. Without the usual cheers that accompanied such sword-play, each and every clash sounded like a death knell to her.

"Did you speak to Halton?" she asked, not able to see Boyd's opponent as he was heavily armed, including a helmet—something Boyd lacked. With nothing more than a tunic of mail, Boyd appeared to her frightfully exposed.

"I did. He asked for you. Said little."

"He fights well," she remarked. Too well. "So the rumors were true?"

"If they were not, I doubt the Englishman would have agreed to this fight."

"He deflects every blow," Galia said, unable to keep the worry from her voice.

"Lord Halton is a skilled swordsman."

As before, Boyd continued to press, nearly never on the defensive. But it seemed to have cost him just then as Halton avoided Boyd's attack.

More so than Boyd?

She left the question unasked, not willing to know the answer.

I promise you, Gal, I will win this duel.

He would keep his promise. He must keep his promise.

How could she have fallen in love with him so quickly when Galia had repeatedly denied herself, denied her suitors, with no more than a pang in her chest even for the most qualified candidates? It had been so easy until now to deny herself.

Easy, until it wasn't.

She gasped and immediately covered her own mouth. 'Twas unlikely Boyd could hear her at this distance, but she would take no chances. Halton had made contact with Boyd's arm. "He's bleeding," Galia said, assuming at first the mail had saved him, but then spotting blood dripping from his forearm.

"Halton's tip found a mark. It happens."

Suddenly she remembered the night Halton and his men first appeared outside their gates. Alan had come to fetch her in the dead of the night. By morn, their tents had been set, the siege declared. Though her heart threatened to beat out of her chest then, as now, a calm had settled over her that did not seem to be coming now. She'd believed herself the victor. Had long prepared for a siege such as the one they'd endured.

How did one prepare to watch the man they loved face death?

I love him.

There was no help, nor recourse, for it. But the truth was more evident now than ever.

"He tires," Alan said beside her. Galia thought he meant Halton, but again, was afraid to ask. Instead she looked at the faces of his men, standing clear across the courtyard from them. Did they appear worried?

Nay, unfortunately, they did not.

"They are well-matched," she said, dreading the words as they came from her own mouth.

"Aye." Alan stepped forward, as if something more were about to happen. In truth, it did. And Galia could no longer witness it. She looked away, dirt and snow mixed below her feet. The sickening clash of swords sounded no longer.

Instead, silence reigned.

CHAPTER 26

Blood dripped from his arm.

Boyd felt as if he'd just engaged two MacCabes at once. The Englishman was both strong and skilled.

But Boyd was more skilled, and a wee bit stronger.

After deflecting Halton's last blow, Boyd wanted this fight ended. He'd seen Galia from the corner of his eye and knew she was likely worried for Gurstelle.

Worried for him.

And so, he ended it. Halton's sword now lay at his feet, the tip of Boyd's lying on his chest. He could not pierce it through his armor, but Boyd could easily cut the man's throat now that he'd been disarmed. They both knew it, yet neither of the men moved.

It was a judicial duel, which meant he was within rights to end Halton's life. Though the other man likely would not have offered mercy, were Boyd's father here to witness this fight, he would expect it from him.

Instead, he offered the choice to Galia.

Without glancing at her, he called out clearly. "'Tis your choice, my lady. Does he live or die this day?"

He knew what her answer would be before she gave it.

"Spare him," Galia called, her voice strong and true.

With two swift motions, Boyd had pulled back his sword and picked up his opponent's. He held both out straight now, lest Halton had thoughts of using the moment to his advantage. Instead, he removed his helm.

The baron stepped back, as did Boyd.

It wasn't until Galia stepped forward that he felt the full force of his victory. Gurstelle was free. Wallace would get his men.

After sparing a quick glance at Boyd's arm, Galia turned to the Englishman.

"You are much younger than is rumored," Galia said.

Boyd could not resist laughing. Indeed, he'd also assumed the man to be older. By his reputation, his standing with the king, and his reputed skill, he'd assumed the man was closer to his father's age and not his own.

"And you," the Englishman said to Galia, "more beautiful than is rumored."

Of all the things that could have come from his mouth, that was the least expected. And most unwelcome. The man who had just laid siege to Gurstelle Castle and attempted to kill him was now . . . flirting with Galia?

Her laugh rang out in the courtyard. "All must appear beautiful to a man whose life was just spared. Will you honor your agreement, my lord?"

"I am a man of honor," the baron said, bowing.

"I would hear an aye or nay," she counted. "If it pleases you?"

There was a mocking to her tone Boyd was unaccustomed to hearing from her. He'd known Galia was a formidable opponent, had heard of her widespread reputation, but to witness it firsthand?

"It pleases me to say, aye, the siege is ended. Your champion was well chosen."

The Englishman locked eyes with Boyd. He could not respect a man who fought for King Edward. Would not do so with a man who'd caused Galia such grief as he had. And yet, the baron fought valiantly. He'd have bested most men, but thankfully, Boyd was not most.

"Tell your king Gurstelle Castle will hold against any man or army he sends against it," she said definitively.

"I assure you he will be swayed from any further notions of seizing upon this path north."

And then, the bastard smiled. Actually smiled at Galia, as if they'd met at court and he was prepared to ask her for a dance.

Boyd had had enough of this. "Go," he said forcefully. "Take your men back to England."

Again, the Englishman looked his way. "You are an even better swordsman than your cousin," he said, surprising Boyd again. "I had the honor of facing him at the Tournament of Kings."

"You knew of me?" he asked.

"I did."

"And accepted the terms anyway?"

The Englishman nodded. "The siege was at an end. 'Twas my only opportunity remaining."

'Twas a pity that a man so skilled would waste his efforts fighting for someone such as King Edward.

"You'd have accepted death so easily?"

The baron smiled as if he'd not nearly been killed that day. "Death comes to us all, Kerr." Then to Galia, "Good day, my lady."

Turning and leaving, without his sword, his men

following close, Halton retreated. Alan looked at Boyd. He nodded.

Chasing Halton down, Alan called to him and handed him the weapon. Halton sheathed it and met Boyd's eye, knowing he could have given the order not to return the sword as his opponent, and left in truth.

"Shall we be certain he makes good on his promise?" Alan asked.

"He will," Boyd said confidently. He might be an Englishman, but a man like Halton would not go back on his word. He was certain of it.

"I will join you in a moment," Galia said to Alan as he and the others made their way toward the gatehouse. "First I would see to Boyd's wound."

The others continued on, leaving Boyd and Galia alone.

He met her eyes, uncertain of the direction of her thoughts.

"You are alive," she said, as if disbelieving it to be so.

"I am." He bowed, as Halton had done. "As promised."

"And injured." She moved to look at his arm. The bleeding had stopped, but that did not seem to satisfy her. "Will you see the surgeon?"

"It does not need—" He amended his response, seeing her expression. "I will see the surgeon."

"Thank you," she said simply.

Somehow, he understood her words had naught to do with his wound or the surgeon. "You are most welcome. Though my motives here were selfish, Galia. As you said"—he could not keep the sarcasm from his voice—"I did it for the cause."

She winced. "Perhaps I was harsh when I said as much. I meant only that you did not fight for me."

"Are you certain of it?"

They were at an impasse.

"Go," he said finally. "The Englishman will, I believe, hold true to his word. But you should join Alan." He stopped, thinking of their duel. "The man was not at all what I'd have expected."

"Nay," she agreed, "he was not."

Boyd would not allow himself the jealousy that was, incredibly, bubbling within him. He'd not comment on the fact that the baron seemed to actually be flirting with her, the woman whose people he'd dragged through the pits of hell these past months.

But he wanted to.

If not Halton, there would be another man come to Gurstelle to make Galia break her precious vow not to marry.

"You are in pain," she said. "Go. We shall speak later."

She thought Boyd scowled because he was in pain. Indeed, he was, but not from the swordfight.

"Thank you," she said again, lifting her skirts to join Alan on the ramparts. The only inclination Boyd gave that he'd heard her was a slight nod of the head.

We shall speak later.

Indeed. And in the meantime, Boyd needed an ale. A tankard of it, for that had been the most difficult fight of his life. In truth, there had been a moment, as he engaged Halton, that his family flashed before him. Boyd had considered, for the first time, that he could lose the duel. That he could indeed die that day.

That thought had led to another. One he did not care to explore at the moment.

So instead, he would drink.

CHAPTER 27

BY THE TIME Galia had witnessed the last of the Englishmen leave her lands, the sun had begun to set. She sent men to assess the damage, which Galia knew already would be extensive. But most importantly . . . they were gone.

Celebrations were well underway. Though she bid those who'd remained within the castle walls throughout the siege to remain, in an abundance of caution, few heeded her words. None would be admitted back inside, she'd warned them, until they could be assured that Halton and every last one of his men had crossed the border into England. The scouts would not return for at least a sennight, but none seemed to care.

Though they'd maintained a supply line throughout the past months, stores would need replenishing. The coin necessary to account for lost incomes would not be aided by Galia losing men to Wallace's battle.

Problems for another day, Alan assured her. Tonight was one to rejoice.

Yet how could Galia celebrate Boyd's leave-taking?

She'd planned to return directly to the hall, but Ada had

intercepted her and insisted she change her gown. So now, the evening meal was well underway.

Though she'd offered for Boyd to sit at the head table, he was with his men instead. Not surprising, as Boyd was not the type of man to relish accolades. But Galia could not stave off a twinge of disappointment. She'd hoped to speak with him this eve, but as she entered the hall, it seemed their discussion would have to wait.

All stood, as if it were she and not Boyd who had been responsible for Halton and his men's departure. She smiled, and gestured toward the man responsible. More cheers, this time for Boyd.

Galia was not so shallow as to care that Boyd had been the one to send Halton back to England, but still, the idea that she'd needed him . . .

Just before she climbed the dais, the man in question navigated away from the bench on which he sat and came to her.

"If the offer still stands?"

"Of course." She gestured for one of the servants to set his place. "On this eve especially, you deserve a place of honor here at Gurstelle."

The sudden quickening of her pulse told Galia all she needed to know of her true feelings for Boyd, as if they'd not been clear to her already when she thought of him dueling Halton.

"I was waiting for you," he said as the cheers began to abate and the musicians, whose instruments had been silent of late, began to play. He held her chair for her, waving her servant away.

"Were you?" she asked, now that they could speak freely without fear of being overheard. The hall, at her bidding, brimmed with the best meats Gurstelle served. Every pitcher and tankard was filled to the brim.

"Indeed."

"This eve or . . . ?" The moment the words left her lips, Galia regretted them. She'd drunk two goblets of wine already in her chamber, sharing them with Ada, who was as joyous as all the rest that Gurstelle's walls were no longer surrounded by Englishmen.

"A lifetime, it seems."

Her hand froze halfway to the goblet. She turned her head toward him. "Boyd," she began, finally reaching for the goblet.

"Your tone is much too serious for a celebration such as this."

"Indeed," she agreed. "I'd been jesting," she said, even if her words were not quite true.

"I had not."

As if he spoke of the meal or the wall hangings, or some other trivial matter and not that of their very relationship to each other, Boyd began to eat. But Galia could not let go of his words. Throughout the meal, every time he glanced her way, every accidental touch of their fingers as she and Boyd shared a trencher, they came back to her.

A lifetime, it seems.

I had not.

By the time Beatrice's legendary cakes and custards were brought out, Galia could not remember the worries that had plagued her these past days.

When Boyd asked if she wished to dance, she was glad for the distraction. Until Galia realized the distraction she needed was from him.

Instead, they moved toward each other, and back, as the music's notes carried throughout the hall. This particular dance required their hands to meet in the air, and when they did, it all rushed back at once in her mind.

That first bath.

His hands beneath the water of her own.

Their night together, Boyd atop her, looking at Galia as if she were a queen. That same body that evaded Halton's sword, that was so well-trained as to withstand more than any other man here in Gurstelle, and well beyond its gates, had moved over hers almost gently.

She wanted that again.

She wanted him again.

But Galia also wanted more from him, and the admission to herself was as shocking as their touch. His hands, so much larger than her own. Hands that could kill a man.

Hands that could make her scream with pleasure.

"If you continue to look at me so, I will scoop you up," he said as they danced. "And take you from this hall, your people's reactions be damned."

If 'twas another man, and not Boyd, out there. Would you be here, in the kitchens?

How she'd fallen in love with him so quickly, Galia would stop questioning. 'Twas done. And now the only question remaining was, what would she do with the knowledge? Boyd did not wish to marry.

And yet, could she simply allow him to leave the moment her men were readied without even inquiring about his feelings?

A lifetime, it seems.

What had he meant by that?

She would find out.

"I would like that," Galia admitted. "Very much."

He stumbled.

And, as in all things, did not hesitate.

It took her a moment to realize Boyd truly meant to walk away from the dancers, and from the hall, in the midst of the celebration. She watched him leave, and then turn, nodding toward the exit of the hall.

Surely their absence would be noticed.

Galia looked around. Perhaps it would not. In truth, she hoped only none were injured this eve, as the celebrations seemed to be only beginning.

They had much to celebrate.

She had much to celebrate.

Galia lifted her skirts and followed Boyd from the hall.

CHAPTER 28

HE'D HARDLY CLOSED the door to Galia's chamber before pulling her toward him.

Every touch. Every look. Every moment this eve in the hall had told him that his vision—of riding away from Gurstelle, never to see Galia again, as he realized just how skilled a swordsman Halton had been—meant precisely what he thought it had.

Did he want to marry?

Nay.

Did he want to put his faith in a woman, as he'd done once before, to have his heart torn in two?

Nay.

Did he know how to serve Wallace and Galia both?

Nay, he did not.

But Boyd was certain of one thing above all. For that brief moment that he had considered meeting death, it was her face he saw. Now, thankfully, she was flesh and blood in his hands. She did not resist as he claimed her mouth, his head slanting to take her fully into him. Their tongues clashed, tangling with need for each other.

He understood the urgency with which Gal attempted to pull his tunic from him. He did the same, untying the many laces at her back without once breaking contact until he was forced to do so, lifting his tunic and discarding it with one quick motion.

"Are you certain?" he asked, untying the laces of his boots with the same speed. Without waiting for her answer, he tossed his boots to the side.

In response to his question, Galia pushed down the gown he'd unlaced. It pooled at her feet, and when she stepped over it, Boyd could not get to her quickly enough. By the time her slippers were off, he'd removed every vestige of his clothing.

Only her shift remained.

He tore that from her body, picked Galia up, and brought her to the bed. Over and over again he saw Halton's sword. The doubt in his own ability to defeat him, though fleeting, clawed at him still. Galia was a reminder that he was very much alive, and he'd never wanted to be with a woman more than this very moment.

They had much to discuss, but as he moved over her, Boyd knew that time was not now.

Her fingers twined through his hair as he kissed her.

Everywhere.

Her lips, her neck.

"Oh," she said as he licked first one nipple, and then the other. Teased them both with his teeth. "I like that," she murmured.

But Boyd couldn't answer her. He was now kissing a trail downward, content only when he captured her womanhood and heard Galia's moans of pleasure, the sweetest music ever made. When he felt her tense, knew Galia's first release was coming, he did not relent.

It would be the first of many this eve.

He was alive. Gurstelle, free.

The woman he loved, beneath him.

"Boyd." She pulled him up to her as the release ran its course. "Please," she begged, though there was no need. He would gladly give Galia what she asked for.

Guiding himself inside her, Boyd held Galia's gaze as his shoulders and arm muscles flexed with the tension of holding himself above her. But he wanted to see her face, the candlelight adequate for such a purpose.

Her lips parted. Galia's eyes closed as he fully pressed into her. When he moved, it was with such purpose that he was certain the words didn't need to be said.

But he did anyway.

"I will not be pulling away from you, Galia."

He circled his hips, the movements slower and more deliberate now than the frantic pace at which they had torn off their clothing. Her fingertips pressed into Boyd's shoulders, as if to grip him. To hold him in place.

"Nay," she said, never turning her gaze from his. "You will not."

Her hips lifted to meet his every thrust.

"If I do not," he continued, "a babe could result." Any remaining doubt, any questions about how such a thing could work, fled as quickly from his mind as they came. He'd wanted one thing in that moment death had greeted him.

It was not freedom from Edward's grasp, as precious as that was to him.

Nor even was it his family, who Boyd loved above all.

Until now.

"You do not wish to marry," she whispered as he

prepared his left arm to support him above her. With the other, he reached down in between them.

"Did not wish to marry," he corrected. "And you?"

As his thumb pressed to her womanhood and began to circle it, Boyd knew he was not playing fair. But he cared little for anything but Galia's response.

"Did not wish for it either," she said. "Until you."

His chest constricted, and then such joy soared through him that Boyd knew for certain what he'd already suspected. As Galia responded to his touch and began to quiver beneath him, he removed his hand, braced himself, and buried himself so fully in her that there could be no question of pulling from her now.

She cried out, Boyd catching her response with his mouth in a kiss that was meant to claim.

And it did.

Allowing his own release to couple with hers, Boyd spilled his seed into her. Having gone from wanting to prevent a babe to willing for one to be born from their coupling this eve, Boyd let himself go so completely, the castle could be under attack and he'd not move to defend it.

He could do nothing but hold her, his heart hammering at a pace he never knew was possible. They were alive, and would not waste such a thing on doubts or, worse, remnants of the past.

When he was able to breathe normally again, Boyd spun them around so as not to crush her, Galia now atop him. Pulling out, knowing it would not be long before he was ready again to love her, Boyd reached up and pushed Galia's hair to the side. He stared at her beautiful face for a time, and then made certain she understood what had just happened.

"We will marry," he said.

Thankfully, she did not disagree.

CHAPTER 29

"I SHOULD HAVE SAID I loved him." Galia paced back and forth, as she'd done for so many days since Boyd had left. "I should have agreed to marry him."

Ada chased her with the hairbrush, attempting to get Galia to sit back down. But she could not do it. Word had reached them of the battle late last eve. With her own men and other borderland clans, Wallace's men, of course, and those sent as mercenaries from the French king, Edward had easily been defeated.

Surprised, defeated, and with luck, not to return to the borderlands for some time. Though Galia was not as hopeful as others about the last. The English king grew angrier at his Northumberland lords, frustrated by the boarders, and indeed, Boyd's own family, and his meddling in Scots affairs was just beginning.

Or so she believed. As did others who saw this as a very temporary victory.

"You did agree to marry him," Ada reminded her.

"Aye, but on his return."

She'd not wished to rush the matter. Neither had Boyd

told her he loved her that night, even though 'twas possible they could have conceived a child. They had spoken of how a marriage between them might be possible. How he could continue to fight for the Scots' cause, continue to remain in Wallace's camp, as her husband.

Such a thing seemed impossible. She said as much, and Boyd had not disagreed. But neither was he willing to relinquish his position in the outlaw's camp, and so they had agreed on nothing. Except, of course, that neither wished for Boyd to leave Gurstelle never to return again.

"Why did you not say it?" Ada asked, not for the first time. They'd had this conversation before, but still, Ada asked the question.

"As I've told you." Galia did sit then. "He did not. And so I did not. I've no better answer than that."

"Then I've no better response than before."

Which was that Ada thought both of them mad.

"'Tis possible to marry without love," Galia said.

"Aye. But not for two people who've sworn never to marry."

"I am stubborn," she said, recognizing now what she should have before.

"Aye," Ada agreed. "Though I do not know his reasons, for I'm certain he loves you as well."

Did he?

Boyd had admitted to being afraid, if only for a moment, during that duel. Had said he'd thought of her, wondered what life they could have had together, in that moment. But he'd not confessed his love, and so neither had she. Instead, they spoke of marriage, of their future.

"What if he was slain?" she asked, the question that had been in her mind each and every day; one Galia rarely voiced aloud.

Knowing nothing Ada could say would console her, feeling poorly for putting her poor maid through the same questions she'd been asking for as many days, Galia was prepared to take back the question when a knock on the door interrupted them.

Ada left the inner chamber and returned a moment later.

"You're needed in the hall, my lady," she said.

Jumping from her seat and responding to "my lady" from the same woman she'd been commiserating with just moments before, Galia neither hesitated nor asked the reason. But the silent exchange between her and her maid told her 'twas not Boyd.

The servant at her door confirmed it.

"There is a visitor, my lady, who wishes to speak with you."

"A visitor?" she asked, about to inquire as to their name when Ada rushed to her side. "Your ring." She handed Galia the ring, one belonging to her mother, that she rarely took from her fingers. Galia had been staring at it as Ada brushed her hair earlier. For reasons she could not explain, she'd removed it and placed it on the wooden table in front of her.

"Put it away," she said now. "With the other jewels."

Her mother adored adornments of all kinds, but Galia preferred fewer, and the ring had never felt quite comfortable on her finger.

It was only when she had made her way to the hall that Galia realized she never did inquire as to the visitor's name. While their gates were open once again, the siege long over and Halton's men not spied this side of the border since the day Boyd had defeated him, 'twas early in the day to receive a guest.

He stood with his back to her at the entrance. But it was not his height nor build, the man nearly as tall and solid as Boyd, that caught Galia's eye. It was those gathered in the hall to break their fast. They acted oddly.

Whispers, she realized. They were talking quietly to each other about something. About her guest, it seemed, as glances his way gave over to standing as they noticed she had appeared. Galia, as she did each day, motioned for those gathered to sit.

The guest, realizing she was behind him, spun toward her.

Galia would have gasped if not for having met Boyd.

Before her was one of the most handsome men she had ever spied. Not as handsome as Boyd, to her, but certainly darker. His hair pitch black. His bow so perfectly executed that he seemed to her akin to royalty.

Not royalty, she realized as he walked toward her. Galia spied the coat of arms on his tunic and wondered how he had come to be here.

And why.

Most importantly, 'twas clear a Waryn had come to grace her hall, but she knew not which one of them stood before her.

"Pardon my early morning arrival," he said, his voice as smooth and deep as Boyd's.

"You are a Waryn," she blurted, her manners seeming to have escaped her. Galia's eyes flew to her steward's, who opened his mouth to introduce their guest.

But he did it first.

"Aye, my lady. Sir Holt Waryn, son of Lord Geoffrey and Lady Sara of Kenshire, at your service."

He was an earl's son, but still he bowed to her.

Holt Waryn. An Englishman. A renowned tourney

fighter. All of Scotland knew of him. But to her, he was one thing above all.

Boyd's cousin.

"Welcome," she said. "Tell me why you've come to Gurstelle Castle."

CHAPTER 30
HOLT

SHE WAS as beautiful as rumored.

It was easy to see why his cousin had fallen for the countess. Holt had been surprised, of course, to learn of it. Boyd lived for the Scots' cause. To serve Wallace when not protecting their family's interests.

Now, he understood. Though it wasn't Lady Galia's beauty alone that convinced Holt what he had heard on the road was more than merely whispers. The woman looked at him with such an absence of fear, it took Holt back momentarily.

"I was but two days' ride from here when I learned of the siege. And my cousin's presence at Gurstelle."

"He is no longer here." Lady Galia spoke softly to a serving girl and then gestured toward the hall's entrance. "The solar, if it pleases you? I will have food and drink brought to us. Your squire and other men are most welcome to break their fast in my hall."

Holt nodded to Oliver, who all but ran to the hall. The boy was too eager by half, but with no parents to speak of, Holt had no choice but to foster him. His own squire had been knighted, and Oliver already followed him from tourney to tourney; Holt had not realized he had no parents, or home, until last summer.

"Why do you pass through?" Lady Galia asked as a servant opened the door to her solar. It was well appointed, and the small table at its center was set for a private meal. Holt sat on the velvet-cushioned seat, grateful for the luxury after so many days of travel. And more ahead of him.

"We ride to Eglinton," he said as she sat across from him.

"Why," she asked, "does an Englishman ride so far north into Scotland during such troubled times?"

Indeed, the food and drink she promised arrived already. Her staff was efficient.

"A tourney," he said.

Lady Galia smiled. "Of course. I should have known."

He seized on the comment. "You know of me from Boyd? 'Tis said he came here before leaving with Gurstelle men to join Wallace in the Battle of Shirston St. Mary?"

"You are well informed, Sir Holt."

If she were not Boyd's woman, he'd have seized upon such a comment, but there would be no flirting with her if the rumors were true. Though Holt sometimes found it difficult to rein in the comments that came freely for other women, especially with one as beautiful as Lady Galia.

"Am I well informed to learn that you and my cousin grew close while he was here, at Gurstelle?"

The eagle-eyed countess's smile faltered. Aye, 'twas true. There was no need for her to answer.

"We are to marry," she said plainly.

Holt stood, all thoughts of the woman's beauty forgotten. He moved to her, knelt at her side, and offered the vow every woman in his family received from him. "I honor you with a vow of protection, of sworn allegiance, and offer my life if 'tis necessary, Lady Galia." Holt would have laid his sword across his knee but it had been taken from him at the entrance to the keep.

It took her a moment, but Lady Galia quickly recovered.

"You are all your cousin has professed," she said, "and I thank you for your words, Sir Holt."

He stood and moved back to his seat. Then, picking up a piece of bread, Holt tore some off and buttered it. Lady Galia ate more delicately, and Holt slowed his pace, remembering his manners. It had been too many days on the road.

"He's not yet returned?" Holt asked.

"Nay," she said, clearly worried.

Holt alleviated her fears. "Boyd will come back. The man is impossible to kill. I've tried."

Her eyes widened. "You've tried to kill your cousin?"

He shrugged. "In a manner, aye. Though not permanently."

The countess laughed. "Death is permanent, or have you not been told as much?"

He'd say nothing of the "little death." Of lovemaking. This was Boyd's woman. But the urge was strong. Holt needed a woman, and soon. But neither would he dishonor Lady Galia by taking one of the serving women here to his bed. He sighed, wondering how much longer the tourney life would serve him.

"I've been told," he said between bites. "Tell me about your courtship."

She did. Lady Galia spoke of how Boyd and the men entered Gurstelle Castle. He was impressed, and Holt was rarely impressed with the feats of men any longer. She told him of the siege, and seemed particularly unhappy about the way that it ended.

175

If there was one thing Holt knew better than how to win a tourney, it was how to peer inside another's mind. He'd done it always, even as a young boy. To him, 'twas nothing more than careful observance. A glance. The movement of another's eyes. The tone of their voice or where they moved their hands.

It was both a blessing, and a curse.

He spoke plainly. "You did not approve of Boyd's duel?"

She seemed embarrassed by the question. "Of course I . . . approve. The siege ended because of it."

The countess lied. Or at least, did not offer her full truth. "However?" he prompted, waiting.

She struggled with her next words. He encouraged her. "If Boyd were here, he would tell you to say the words that do not come easily from your lips. For if you do not"—he smiled—"I will learn them anyway."

It was true. Boyd would say such a thing. He would also be quite appalled that Holt had an opportunity to speak to his betrothed alone before she was properly warned of him. Holt supposed he deserved such a reputation.

"I did not—do not—wish to need a man to save Gurstelle," she said finally.

Though Lady Galia seemed surprised by her own honesty, Holt was not. Such free speaking was a trait most he spoke with shared.

"Gurstelle would have been lost long ago, I am certain, if not for your leadership. You've naught to fear from having my cousin at your side. He is as honorable, and more loyal, as any man."

She blinked. Still, there was something amiss.

"Tell me," he said, finished chewing.

"I do not know you," she began, but Holt pushed away her concerns.

"I will be family soon. Your favorite of all Boyd's cousins. Tell me," he said again.

When Lady Galia finished laughing, she seemed as if she might actually tell him what concerned her, something about Boyd, he was certain, but she never had the opportunity.

The door opened once again, and the very man they spoke of filled its frame.

"This," he said, looking directly at Holt with his lips tugging upward, "is not at all how I envisioned"—Boyd turned his attention to Galia—"our reunion."

CHAPTER 31

HE REFUSED to be jealous of Holt.

But when Boyd came into the chamber—the journey back to Gurstelle having seemed the longest of his life—it was not, as he said, the reunion he'd expected.

Of all his cousins, Holt would be the one he'd least wish for Galia to meet alone. Before they were married. He trusted both Holt and Galia implicitly, but the uncertainty that clawed its way into his head as he opened the door was one he could not ignore.

Proof, if he needed it, that he'd made the right decision. One he would share with Galia as soon as they were alone.

Both of them stood, and since the door closed behind them, Boyd didn't hesitate. He strode to Galia, pulled her to him, and kissed her so thoroughly as not to be even slightly proper. He'd missed her dearly, and from her response, it seemed she felt the same.

When he finally released her, Boyd turned to his cousin, who looked at him with such an expression of amusement that Boyd could not resist laughing. As it was so often with

Holt, none could remain angry with him. Not that Boyd was angry. Just . . .

Goddammit. Jealous.

What an appalling state.

"You are a right bastard," Boyd said as he embraced his cousin. "I thank you for entertaining Galia in my stead."

The comment was meant to be sarcastic, but of course Holt did not take it as such.

"My pleasure, cousin," he said, slapping him on the back and taking his seat once again.

"Did you break your fast?" Galia asked him.

"Nay, but a setting is being—"

A knock on the door interrupted him. A trencher was set beside Galia, and Boyd explained as he sat that he had traveled throughout the night to reach Gurstelle the moment he was able to leave the battle.

"Edward's forces had no chance for success," he said. "They were overwhelmed from the start, and retreated more quickly than we could have hoped."

"My men?" Galia asked, worry etched on her face.

"All spared. There were few casualties, as William sent his own men against Edward's first."

"Meaning you," she responded, looking both relieved and worried yet again.

"Aye," he admitted. "But I am here," he reminded her. And then, unable to wait, Boyd added, "And here I will remain."

He was uncertain whether Galia or Holt was more surprised by the news.

"I told William 'twould be my last campaign with him as a member of his inner circle, but certainly not the last I will fight against Edward. But now that the king is aware of

King Philip's support of our cause, I fear the repercussions will be fierce."

"They will," Holt admitted. "But I must admit to some surprise that you so easily relinquished your place by Wallace's side."

Boyd looked at Galia. Her eyes were wide, swimming with unshed tears.

Do not cry, my love.

"Perhaps," Holt amended, "I am not surprised at all."

"It will not be the last battle," Boyd warned Galia. "But if you will still have me, I would remain at Gurstelle by your side."

"As Earl of Gurstelle," she reminded him.

A title he neither coveted nor cared about. "I leave my English cousins to covet titles we've little use for if Scotland falls into the hands of," he addressed Holt, "your king."

"In name only," Holt teased back. "I serve none but myself," he said, unapologetic as always.

"You serve Kenshire," Boyd reminded his cousin. "And the Brotherhood," he added, referring to the union between both of their families.

"I do," Holt admitted. "Though not as faithfully as some."

At Galia's expression of curiosity, he explained. "I am a tourney knight. A third son, not destined for title nor inheritance."

Boyd made a sound. "You will inherit Hillston Manor." He explained to Galia, "A castle in all but name. It sits just south of the border between Kenshire and Merchwood."

Holt dismissed him. "I've no need of a manor house."

"And this," he continued to Galia, "is my cousin Holt. He has no need of a manor house, his reputation as the greatest tourney player on the isle more important for him to uphold. Instead he prefers to lament his status as a third son for your sympathy."

Holt nearly spit out his ale. "For sympathy? I do no such thing."

Galia tried not to laugh. "I am glad," she said, clearly having fallen under Holt's spell, as all who met him did, "you've come to Gurstelle, Sir Holt. You've proven quite entertaining."

Wretched jealousy. Boyd ignored the pang in his chest. He would not be one of those men.

"Will you remain for the wedding?"

That jolted him from his review.

"The wedding," both he and Holt said simultaneously.

"Aye, the wedding. I thought to speak privately with you on the matter," she said to Boyd. "But now that you've returned, I thought perhaps . . ." She took a deep breath.

He answered without waiting for her to finish. "Aye," he said. "This eve? Tomorrow? Name a day, my lady, and it will be done."

He was rewarded with her smile.

"How long can you remain?" she asked his cousin.

"A sennight, but no more."

"What say you, Boyd?" she asked.

"I say . . ." He had so much to tell her. So much to say. "'Tis time for Holt to see to his men."

"I've only Oliver with me."

"Oliver then," Boyd said, knowing Holt understood well he wished to be with Galia alone. But, as expected, Holt would not be easily accommodating.

"Oliver is in the hall, well taken care of, I'm certain."

Galia did laugh then, and Boyd watched as she looked back and forth between them with amusement. Every moment since he'd been away, he thought of her face. Her touch. Wished to be back here at Gurstelle with her.

This time he was less gentle. "Out. Now."

Holt pressed his lips together, still smiling. But he stood, at least. "As you wish, oh future Earl of Gurstelle, my esteemed cousin and most valued member of our family."

He bowed then, first to Galia and then Boyd. The gesture was as unnecessary as it was amusing, but Boyd would not let Holt see him smile. It was only after his cousin took his leave that Boyd did so, even more broadly as he thought of the reunion he'd wished to have.

"Do you have the key for this chamber?" he asked, standing once again.

"I do," she said. "And I aim to use it."

CHAPTER 32

THE MOMENT the solar door was locked, Boyd kissed her even more thoroughly than before. His tongue tangled with hers, their bodies pressed against one another, and Galia was glad he wore no tunic.

When she reached between them, lifting the linen shirt, Boyd guided her hand to him. His trews open enough that she could wrap her fingers around him, Galia relished the sounds she elicited from him. He was hard, so ready for her, and Galia did not wish to wait.

"I want to feel you inside me," she said, breaking their kiss.

His nostrils flared. Then, without another word, he spun her around and unlaced her gown so quickly that Galia had little chance to recover before he turned her back to him.

"Oh," she said as he lifted first her shift, and then her.

"Wrap your legs around me," he said, not taking his eyes from hers.

She did.

"How do you hold me so easily with one—"

Her words were cut short as his fingers found her. Galia gripped onto his shirt with both hands.

"So wet for me," he murmured, moving his finger perfectly within her.

"Please," she begged. "I've missed you, Boyd."

It seemed she would not have to ask again. He pulled his hand from her and guided himself into her, the feeling of fullness growing as he did.

"'Tis so different this way," she said when Boyd began to move. But it was Galia that decided how quickly. Which way to circle her hips. When his lips found hers again, she marveled at his strength but had little time for thoughts of anything but the growing urgency building within her.

Each night while he was away, Galia had dreamed of this, of being with him again. She began to tremble, and then was so completely overtaken that his own cries were melded with hers as they found release together.

She could no longer kiss him, the sensations too great and Galia's need to understand what had just happened between them something she wished to think fully on. Dropping her chin to his shoulder, she held on. Breathed in his scent. Remained a part of him until Boyd pulled out and then repositioned her, though her legs were still wrapped around his waist.

It occurred to her finally that he might be tiring, and so she pulled her head up to ask.

But instead of finding the question, she discovered something else entirely. Boyd watching her, looking at her in what could only be described one way.

"You seemed unbothered to name me as Earl of Gurstelle," he said softly.

She sighed, thinking of Margo's words. And even of his

cousin's. "We will rule here together," she said. "I've no doubt of it."

"Nor should you, Galia."

She blinked. "You are truly not returning to Wallace's camp?" When they had spoken before, he'd talked of moving between Gurstelle and Ettrick Forest. Of being her husband but also Wallace's confidant. And though 'twas not ideal, neither could Galia risk having Boyd leave for battle never to return again.

"I still believe in the cause," he said. "But I love you more." Her chest swelled. "I rue the day I left without saying as much, and can only count myself half a coward," he said. "Facing one of the best swordsmen I've ever challenged was naught compared to loving again, Galia. But 'tis so plain to me that you must think me a fool to have questioned us so."

"Nay," she said. "Not a fool. As I held back as well. The thought of saying 'I love you' and not hearing the same in return . . ."

His eyes softened.

"I love you," she said. "So very much."

He kissed her once again. "I risked my life to come here, and would do it again to have met you. It will be my honor to call myself your husband."

How could she have thought herself weaker for needing a man such as Boyd?

"And I," she said, "your wife."

GET BOOK BONUSES

Not ready for the story to end?

Go beyond the HEA with a bonus scene by subscribing to become a CM Insider.

Subscribe at CeceliaMecca.com/Insider

EPILOGUE

"I BEG you to let me taste it."

As she'd done before, Margo shooed her back as if she were not the countess. As if Galia could not simply demand a taste of the first quince pie of the summer. But Margo insisted she wait for the pies to be completed.

She'd not do any such thing, of course. But she did wait until Margo turned her back and scooped up a pewter spoon, prepared to use it even at the risk of incurring Margo's wrath, until Beatrice came into the kitchens carrying her daughter.

Galia immediately dropped a spoon and went to her, holding out her hands. Beatrice gave the babe to her as Margo first peered over Galia's shoulder, smiled at the wee one, and then promptly told the women to get out of her kitchens as the midday meal was being prepared.

Obeying, as one did with the cook, Galia moved into the corridor as the steward's daughter looked sheepishly at her.

"Go on," Galia said. She sensed Beatrice wished to ask her something.

"I just thought . . ." Beatrice shook her head. "Nay, I could not ask such a thing."

Galia gave her a look that made Beatrice immediately change her mind.

"You are so kind to her," Beatrice said. "And will make such a wonderful mother."

Trying not to smile, Galia thought, as she had for many days, what Boyd might say when she told him the news. They would indeed, become parents. With luck he would return soon, as Galia could not wait to share her joy with him. He'd gone to Kenshire for a council after they received word King Edward was so wroth with the Waryns that he'd been threatening to strip the earl and countess of their titles. According to Boyd, the English king had never quite recovered from his anger when their eldest son Hayden married a woman of his bidding, only to ask the woman to spy for him. When she refused after they were wed, King Edward had been angry enough to threaten the Waryn family, and relations with them had not improved since.

He was becoming desperate to subdue the Scots and the situation had become dangerously unstable.

"If God grants me a babe someday," she said now, "I will cherish him, or her, with all my heart."

As they spoke, voices from the courtyard above reached them. They grew louder and louder, so Galia handed the wee babe to her mother, lifted her skirts, and fled up the stairs and into the bright midday sun.

"He is returned, my lady," a young knight said as she realized the voices were her people coming from every building into the courtyard. They climbed to the ramparts to watch, apparently, as the Earl of Gurstelle returned.

Boyd was as beloved here as she. Sometimes, Galia thought, even more so, as his even temperament was the calm they needed. As she too made her way to higher ground to see if the claims were true, Galia spotted her marshal doing the same.

"Is he returned?" she asked Alan, who stood at a parapet in front of her.

"He is." Alan pointed into the distance. She saw nothing there.

"'Tis but grass and hills," she said. "Though no tents."

"Look closer, my lady."

She squinted, lifting her hand up to shield the sun. They were hardly perceptible, but there nonetheless. "I see them."

At Alan's insistence, Boyd had gone with a contingency of men. As they watched, two, and then four, and six, riders came into view.

Her skin tingled, a rush of pleasure making its way from Galia's toes to her cheeks. She could feel them growing warm as she thought of their night together before he left. Thinking of their reunion.

"You've done well, my lady," Alan said.

His candor took her by surprise. As Boyd grew closer and closer to them, she focused instead on her marshal. A man that had been the closest Galia had gotten to a father. "Indeed," she said, "he is quite a man." In many ways.

"Kerr is that, but 'tis not what I meant, my lady."

"Did you not?"

"With him by your side, I've no doubt Gurstelle will flourish despite its position along the border. But you led us here, before he came."

"My mother," she began, but he stopped her.

"Was a fine woman, but not half the countess her daughter has proven to be. You've taken her counsel but learned to discard some of it as well. 'Tis your ability to accept others' advice that has set you apart, Galia, and I'm proud to serve you."

She wrapped her hands around Alan's shoulders. Knowing he was not comfortable with such affection, but not caring, she smiled into his tunic as he squeezed her back.

"I could not have done it without you," she said truthfully as they parted.

Rewarded with a rare smile from Alan, it was not until cheers rose from around them that she realized Boyd and his men had come through the outer gatehouse and were now approaching the inner courtyard.

He was looking up at her.

Though she could not see every detail on his face yet, she sensed his eyes on her. Bigger than the other men, he sat so tall and proud, Galia wondered how she'd not fallen in love with him the very moment she'd first seen him.

"Stay," Alan said as she began to make her way down to greet Boyd. "I will send him here."

It was that kind of quiet thoughtfulness that Galia only now realized she'd learned from Alan. Most saw him as gruff and unrelenting, but small gestures told her the marshal loved her, and their people.

She looked out to the fields—the blessedly empty fields —and tried not to think of the days ahead. Would there be another siege? An attack? Would Edward bring his wrath toward the Brotherhood to their gates?

Galia thought of her mother then. Alan was right. Some of her counsel, like marrying no man, was misguided. But much of it had made Galia the woman she had become. If she were here now, her mother would scold Galia for such thoughts, bidding her to replace them with another.

What if all is well? Think on that, daughter, instead of what might go wrong.

"So deep in thought."

She spun, ran to him, and Boyd lifted her from the ground. He held her, kissed her, Galia returning his kisses and relishing in his all-encompassing embrace.

When he finally put her back down, Boyd pulled back his hands on her shoulders, and looked at her as if he'd never seen her face before.

"How did I come here to aid Wallace and end up with a lass of my own? One I never realized I needed so badly?"

"You snuck in," she reminded him. "Dangerously so, if you'll remember."

"Aye," he said, "I remember it well. And will take no such chances with my life now that I am a husband."

Her smile grew. "Husband," she said, her hand moving to her stomach. "And father."

Boyd's expression just then, of such joy and love, was one Galia would never forget in all her days.

Aye, what if all is well? Think on that, Galia.

And it was.

ABOUT THE AUTHOR

Cecelia Mecca is the author of medieval romance, including the Border Series, and sometimes wishes she could be transported back in time to the days of knights and castles. Although the former English teacher's actual home is in Northeast Pennsylvania where she lives with her husband and two children, her online home can be found at Cecelia-Mecca.com. She would love to hear from you.

- Subscribe to be a CM Insider to receive book news and updates via email.

Connect with Cecelia on:

Also by Cecelia Mecca

Brotherhood of the Border

Kissed by the Knight

A Noble Betrayal

A Clan of Her Own

Son of a Rogue

To Love a Warrior

Border Series

The Ward's Bride: Prequel Novella (free)

The Thief's Countess

The Lord's Captive

The Chief's Maiden

The Scot's Secret

The Earl's Entanglement

The Warrior's Queen

The Protector's Promise

The Rogue's Redemption

The Guardian's Favor

The Knight's Reward

Box Set 1 (Books 1-3)

Box Set 2 (Books 4-6)

Box Set 3 (Books 7-10)

Order of the Broken Blade

Kingdoms of Meria

Time Travel

CONTEMPORARY ROMANCE

Boys of Bridgewater

PARANORMAL ROMANCE

Bloodwite